DIAL M FOR MENNONITE

AMISH COZY MYSTERY

ETTIE SMITH AMISH MYSTERIES
BOOK TWENTY-EIGHT

SAMANTHA PRICE

CHAPTER 1

*E*ttie moved slowly about the living room, tidying things more out of habit than necessity. After she was satisfied of a job well done, she petted her small dog Snowy before she settled into her well-loved couch. It gave a familiar squeak, a sound as comforting as an old hymn.

"I feel a bit odd today," Ettie murmured.

"You are old." Elsa-May chuckled as she continued her one purl and one plain.

"No. I said I feel *odd* today not old."

"Oh, odd. How is that different from any other day?" Elsa-May paused her knitting and looked at Ettie over the top of her knitting spectacles.

Ettie hardly seemed to notice her sister's words as she was caught up in an emotion she couldn't quite place. Her eyes were clouded as they stared out the window. "Yes. I don't know why or what it is. I just feel a bit sad." Ettie's voice was soft, almost drowned out by the gentle patter of rain starting to tap against the windowpane. "Dismal just like the gray sky."

"That's why you need to start knitting. You like needlework so why don't you do that?"

"I could."

"Where's your sampler?" Elsa-May inquired.

"I finished it two years ago. There it is up on the wall." Ettie nodded toward the framed sampler, protected by glass, and read from it. "'To everything, there is a season, and a time to every purpose under the heaven...'"

"Do go on," said Elsa-May.

"I will if you'll stop interrupting." Ettie's voice filled the room, the familiar verse from Ecclesiastes lending a sort of anchor to her drifting spirit. "'A time to be born, and a time to die; a time to plant, and a time to pluck up that which is planted...'" With each line, Ettie felt the heaviness lifting, the timeless words a reminder of life's ebb and flow, and the promise that no sorrow lasts forever.

Elsa-May couldn't help herself. "'A time to weep, and a time to laugh; a time to mourn, and a time to dance...'"

When Elsa-May finished, Ettie felt lighter. "I do like that one."

"That was lovely, Ettie. And through all those times we have each other. Now do you feel better?"

"A little."

Elsa-May made tsk tsk sounds. "You need a hobby. Helping others is always a way to lift one's mood. Why don't we go visiting and see if you can help someone with something?"

Ettie looked over at her sister, slightly envious at the way her knitting gave her a purpose. "Who would I help, and what would I help them with?"

"I don't know. It was just a suggestion. I don't have all the answers under the sun. I'm not a soothsayer."

Ettie looked over at her sister. "Don't you ever feel a bit sad?"

"No because I'm too busy knitting for all my charities to worry about how I'm feeling. Whenever my mind wanders, I think about all the people who'll benefit from these items I'm knitting. You're always looking out the window so why don't you take up bird watching?"

"I already do watch the birds whenever I see them."

"I know, but I mean do it as a serious hobby. Look at the different types of birds that visit us and at what time of day and all that."

Ettie nodded. "Hmm. I like the sound of that, but I don't know if I'd like trekking through the woods trying to find where they live. I could do it from the comfort of my house, like you said." Ettie slumped onto the couch and Kelly, the kitty, jumped up on Ettie's lap. "I think you've struck on a good idea, Elsa-May—bird watching. I need to get out of this mood, but at the same time, I don't feel like doing it. It's what they call a vicious cycle."

"Don't you think you're too old to ride a bicycle?"

Ettie frowned at her sister. "I said cycle, not bicycle. Ah, don't worry. The only thing about bird watching is who is it going to help? I like it that your knitting helps people."

Elsa-May kept knitting, clicking her knitting needles together. "I know what you mean, but the point is, you'll have to leave the house if you want to help someone. No one is just going to knock on our door. Any fool would know that."

The knock on the door was a soft, almost apologetic intrusion, yet it was enough to shock the sisters.

Ettie couldn't help the mischievous spark that ignited in her eyes. "No one is going to knock, eh? The door isn't knocking by itself."

"Well, see who it is, Ettie. Don't just sit there."

"Why is it always me who has to answer the door?" Ettie grunted as she got to her feet.

"Because people always tend to arrive when I'm in the middle of a row of knitting. Alright, I've just finished my row. We'll go together." Elsa-May set her knitting down and they both moved toward the door, curiosity helping them move faster than normal.

When the door opened, they saw an *Englisher*. A lone figure, his hat, worn by the elements, shadowed a face marked with fatigue, and his brown overcoat, despite its wear, clung to him like a protective layer.

"Good morning." He greeted them with a nod. "I'm Gideon Friesen I hope I'm not intruding, but I'm in need of help."

"Help?" Elsa-May repeated.

Out of the corner of her eye, Ettie saw Elsa-May staring at her.

The man continued, "I heard about you both, and I'm here to ask for your advice if you don't mind. I would be ever so grateful if you would take a moment to hear what I've got to say."

Ettie gave him a nod. "Hello, nice to meet you. I'm—"

Elsa-May cut her sister off. "Who told you about us?"

"A young lady who came into my Antique store. I believe her name was Angela. She said people in her community go to you when they have things that just don't add up. She was sure you wouldn't mind helping."

Ettie and Elsa-May looked at each other. "We don't know anyone by the name of Angela. One of my nieces is called Angela but she lives hundreds of miles away."

"The young lady told me she's married to one of your grandsons." He looked from one of the sisters to the other.

"Ah," Elsa-May said, "That would be Ava."

"Yes, that's right. She has two young boys. She's a regular customer and she bought a copper jug last time she was there. Ah, copper, now I could delve into some

5

stories about all the copper items I've had over the years. And how much they've gone up in value. If only I'd kept them all."

Elsa-May moved aside. "Please, come in, Mr. Friesen. We'll help if we can."

After they introduced themselves, they ushered him into the living room.

Once settled on the couch, he removed his hat, setting it aside as he ran a hand through his silver hair. He then looked at them. "I was a Mennonite until a few years ago. Well, many decades ago."

"That's interesting. And why did you leave?" Ettie asked hoping she wasn't being too intrusive.

"I fell in love. We only lasted a few years, sadly."

"We're sorry to hear that, Mr. Friesen."

"Please call me Don. Everyone calls me Don. I didn't go back to my community because... it's complicated. But that's nothing to do with why I'm here today."

"Would you like a cup of hot tea, Don?" Ettie asked.

"No thank you. I hope I'm not disturbing you."

"We're happy to help, aren't we, Elsa-May?"

"It depends on what it is. Can you tell us a little more?"

Snowy and Kelly observed the unfolding scene from a safe distance.

"I'm not sure where to start," Don said rubbing his forehead.

Ettie leaned forward, her eyes gleaming with curiosity. "Why not start at the beginning? It's always the best place."

Don took a deep breath, his eyes scanning the room as if searching for the right words. "It's a rather peculiar incident that occurred yesterday morning at the bakery next door to my antique store."

Ettie's eyes widened, her interest fully captured. "We're listening."

Don cleared his throat. "Next door to my antique shop, is a bakery. Now the baker, a lovely woman, Adele Henderson is her name, discovered a small, intricately crafted key in the middle of a loaf of bread."

Ettie raised an eyebrow, her mind already buzzing with possibilities. "A key, you say? That's certainly an intriguing discovery. Any idea what it might unlock?"

Don shook his head. "None at all, I'm afraid. The key doesn't resemble any I've seen before, and its purpose remains a mystery."

Ettie leaned back as Elsa-May took over the conversation. "You want us to find out what the key unlocks? It could be anything and it could be anywhere. I'm sorry you wasted your time, but I don't see how we'll be able to help at all."

Don nodded in agreement, the lines in his face deepening with his frown. "I understand the absurdity of the task, ladies. But you see, there's more to the story. Mrs. Henderson believes the key wasn't a mistake or a random occurrence. She's convinced it was deliberately placed in her bread dough. What made up her mind about that was the note she found in her kitchen that goes along with it."

Ettie couldn't contain her curiosity. "A note in the bread. Fascinating."

"Close to the bread maybe. I'm not totally certain where the note was found."

"What did the note say?" Elsa-May asked.

"It was a riddle of sorts," Don explained, pulling a crumpled piece of paper from his coat pocket. He unfolded it carefully, as though it were a fragile relic from another time. "It says, *'In the heart where warmth does stay, the hidden passage leads the way. Seek the place where shadows dance, a legacy left to chance.'*"

The sisters exchanged glances, the silent communication of years gone by passing between them. It was clear they were both intrigued and slightly skeptical.

"That does sound like a riddle," Elsa-May murmured.

Ettie stared at the paper. "Is that the actual paper that was found?"

"That's the one."

It had faint blue lines as though it had been pulled from a notebook. "It's been a while since we've encountered a good mystery, or any kind of mystery hasn't it, Elsa-May? I say we help Mr. Friesen with this."

Elsa-May sighed. "I don't think so, Ettie. I'm sorry Don, but it seems like a harmless prank."

Ettie frowned at Elsa-May. "Weren't you just saying that I—"

"Yes, you need something to do with your time, Ettie, and we both agreed that you'd take up bird watching."

Don grinned. "A splendid pastime. In my store I have an excellent pair of binoculars that will do that trick just nicely."

"Oh good. I'd love to take a look at them." Ettie then looked over at Elsa-May. "We can help Don and I can start bird watching. What do you say, Elsa-May?"

Ettie and Don stared at Elsa-May, waiting for her to say yes.

"Very well, but it's one of those mysteries that might never be solved. Where would we even start?"

Don looked between the two sisters, obviously relieved by their willingness to investigate. "I was hoping you might provide some guidance on that. You're both well-known for your keen insights and problem-solving skills, that is, according to my customer. The riddle must be the key to deciphering the key's purpose. I have always had an interest in keys, but this one is so different from any I've seen before."

Ettie's mind raced. "The heart where warmth does stay... that could symbolize a number of things. A hearth in a home, perhaps? Or somewhere central to community life?"

"And the part about shadows dancing," Elsa-May

9

added thoughtfully, "That sounds like it might refer to someplace with flickering lights, or where people gather for events, maybe?"

They pondered in silence for a moment, the only sound was Snowy making low growling noises at their guest.

"Perhaps we should pay a visit to this bakery," Ettie suggested. "Seeing the place where the key was found might provide some inspiration. And we can speak with Mrs. Henderson directly to understand how she found the key and where the note was found."

Elsa-May nodded in agreement. "A practical first step. But we must also consider the safety implications. If this key was deliberately placed, we don't know the intentions behind it. Caution will be essential. It might have been a prank, but maybe not a harmless prank."

Don placed his hat back on. "I could drive you both if you are ready to leave now. Mrs. Henderson is a kind-hearted woman, and I know she'd appreciate any help in finding out what this is about. I can tell you she's unsettled by it all."

"Well, Mr. Friesen, it seems we have ourselves a mystery to solve. Elsa-May, what do you say?"

"Agreed, Ettie. Let us follow this trail of bread-crumbs and see where it leads." Elsa-May chuckled over her breadcrumbs comment seeing they were about to visit a bakery, but Ettie wasn't going to be outdone.

"It'll save us from loafing about. We'll have to rise

to the occasion because this mystery doesn't sound like it's going to be a piece of cake." Ettie grinned at her sister and all Elsa-May did was shake her head.

Mr. Friesen didn't seem to notice. He put his hat back on and got to his feet. "Let's go, shall we?"

CHAPTER 2

*T*heir destination, the bakery, stood at the heart of the town, its windows showcasing an array of delectable treats.

"Oh, it's a café as well," Elsa-May said.

"It is. I get my coffee from here every morning," Don told them as he held the heavy glass door open for them.

As they entered, the tantalizing scent of freshly baked bread and freshly brewed coffee welcomed them.

Mrs. Henderson came out and was introduced to them. She was a kind-faced woman with a flour-dusted apron. "This incident has left me shaken, and I'm eager to find some answers. Who left the key here and the note and why?"

"If you'll excuse me, ladies. I'll head back to my store."

"We'll come and see you before we go," Ettie said.

13

Don gave them a nod before he headed out the door.

"Can you show us the loaf of bread in question?" Elsa-May asked.

Mrs. Henderson led them to a counter where a loaf of bread, carefully preserved under a glass dome, awaited their examination. The loaf, its crust golden and inviting, bore a small label with the date of its creation—yesterday's date. Nestled within the bread, visible through a small window, was the mysterious key, its intricate design captivating their eyes.

"Oh, you left the key in the bread?" Ettie asked.

"I did."

Elsa-May leaned closer, her breath fogging the glass as she studied the key. "From what I can see of the key it is a truly remarkable piece. It's craftsmanship speaks of careful workmanship and attention to detail."

Ettie turned to Mrs. Henderson. "Have you noticed anything out of the ordinary in the past few days? Any peculiar customers or unusual events?"

Mrs. Henderson furrowed her brow, deep in thought. "Now that you mention it, there was a customer who caught my attention a couple of days ago. He was a tall man, wearing a long coat and a hat that partially concealed his face. He didn't say much, just requested a loaf of bread and left in a hurry."

"Did you notice anything else about this man, Mrs. Henderson? Any distinguishing features or peculiar behavior?"

Mrs. Henderson shook her head, her eyes filled with frustration. "I'm afraid not. He was rather nondescript, and I didn't think much of it at the time. But now, with this mystery unfolding, I can't help but wonder if there's a connection. Most of my customers are regulars and he looked as though he was from out of town."

Ettie placed a comforting hand on Mrs. Henderson's shoulder. "We'll ask Mr. Friesen if he saw the same man. Can we examine the key closely and see if it holds any clues?"

"Yes." Mrs. Henderson lifted the glass dome and then handed Ettie a magnifying glass. After that, she handed Ettie the key.

Ettie held it delicately, turning it over in her hands, and then examined it under the magnifying glass. "There are intricate engravings on this key. Symbols and patterns that might hold some significance. We need to figure out what they mean. At first glance, they appear to be a decoration, but I think they are more than that. I think these marks have a meaning, or meanings."

Elsa-May nodded. "Do you have a paper and pen, Mrs. Henderson? We'll write down the symbols and see what connections we can make. Perhaps we can cross-reference them with historical references from the library."

"Oh, now that would be a good idea." Mrs. Henderson handed them a pen and paper from beneath the counter, and with a furrowed brow, Elsa-May carefully sketched the strange symbols.

"I think you're right, Ettie. These markings must mean something. They look old, possibly ancient," Elsa-May added.

They asked Mrs. Henderson more questions, trying to discern any details they might have missed, but the baker had little else to add.

"Does Mr. Friesen know that there are symbols on the key?"

"I'm not certain. He seemed as puzzled as I was when I showed him the key, but I didn't mention the symbols and neither did he. They are rather small so it's possible that he didn't see them."

"I wonder if he might know what these symbols represent. He might know the origin of them seeing he works with antiques," Ettie said.

"We'll show them to him now, then." Elsa-May gave a nod as she held the piece of paper.

"Now where was the note found?"

Mrs. Henderson's eyes opened wide. "Oh, you've seen the note?"

"Yes. Don brought it with him when he visited the house."

"I see. I found it on the counter. I don't see how anyone could've put it there unless they had broken into the place. Or possibly sneaked in while I was doing the baking. My staff doesn't start until a couple of hours after me, and I don't always lock the door."

Ettie nodded. "Interesting."

"How did Don seem to you? Was he worried at all?"

"No. He just wanted to get to the bottom of it."

"I'm just a little unnerved about this whole thing. It's made me feel like someone's watching me. I do appreciate the both of you trying to get to the bottom of it. It is a little unnerving and I'm not sure why. It could be nothing much at all. I mean, the poem could've been accidently left by a customer and the key... I'm not sure how that could've gotten into the bread, but then that becomes a huge coincidence, a poem about a key and then how I found the key. Oh, I hope I didn't worry Don too much about it. Maybe I should've kept the information to myself."

"We'll do what we can to help," Ettie assured her. "We'll be back later."

They thanked Mrs. Henderson and left the bakery.

As they made their way to the antique shop next door, Elsa-May looked over at Ettie. "I still think this is all nonsense, you know. But if it keeps you from moping around, then I suppose it's worth it."

Ettie bristled at her sister's words. "You didn't have to agree to it, Elsa-May. And for your information, something like this is exactly what makes life interesting. A key deliberately baked into a loaf of bread with a riddle and mysterious symbols inscribed into the key is most certainly out of the ordinary. Who put the key there? Was it baked in there, or inserted there after baking?"

Elsa-May sighed. "Okay, it's a mystery, I'll give you that much, but it's not like someone's been murdered."

They reached the antique shop, a quaint establishment that Don Friesen had run for years. The sign hanging above the entrance swayed gently in the breeze, the door beneath it standing slightly ajar.

The immediate scent that greeted them was a mixture of aged wood, the mustiness of old books, and a faint hint of metallic rust. Dim lighting from ornate, hanging fixtures cast a warm glow through the room, making the environment feel even more densely packed.

The aisles were narrow, created by towering shelves laden with everything from Victorian-era figurines and vintage globes to brass telescopes and porcelain dolls with glassy, watchful eyes. Here and there, ornate mirrors with flaking gilt frames reflected their surroundings, contributing to the sense of endlessness clutter and chaos.

Directly beneath their feet, the wooden floorboards creaked with a rhythmic nostalgia, responding with a groan or a squeak to every step the sisters took. Around them, the walls were almost invisible, hidden behind antique tapestries, old paintings with darkening varnish, and an assortment of historical weaponry and agricultural implements.

"Oh, Ettie, I could spend hours in here just looking around. The air itself hums with history, each article a silent witness to the life cycle of objects and their previous owners."

"That's lovely and you're right. Everything has its cycle." Ettie moved to the back of the store where glass cabinets housed a mesmerizing array of jewelry, ancient coins, and delicate curiosities such as lockets, pocket watches, each shimmering softly in the muted light, enticing any observer to lean closer.

"Oh look. Here are the field glasses he was talking about." Ettie picked up the small binoculars and studied them. Then she hung them around her neck. "Seems like a good deal for twenty dollars."

"Oh, Ettie, you can't wear them until you pay for them."

"I'll pay for them in a minute. Don won't mind."

"You don't know that for sure. We just met him this morning."

Ettie looked at Elsa-May through the glasses and then stepped back in shock. "Oh my. That gave me a fright."

"Stop it, Ettie. Behave yourself. Now, where is Don?"

"I don't know. Mr. Friesen!" Ettie yelled out.

Elsa-May clutched her ears with a grimace. "That was absolutely deafening."

Ettie smiled. "Well, at least now we know you aren't going deaf."

"I might be after that racket," Elsa-May retorted,

rubbing her ears. She shot a look at Ettie, who was already moving towards the deeper part of the store.

Ettie raised her voice again. "Mr. Friesen? Don? It's Ettie and Elsa-May calling."

Elsa-May added, "Hello, are you there?"

The response was nothing but silence, punctuated only by the ticking of several antique clocks that filled the room.

"Perhaps he's somewhere in the back." Elsa-May glanced at Ettie, who nodded in agreement.

As Ettie scanned the room, her eyes landed on a telephone lying off its cradle. Curious, she walked over and picked up the receiver. "Hello?" When she heard no one there, she hung up the phone. "No one there."

"You probably startled them. They were possibly on hold for Don while he's getting information on their layaway status," Elsa-May speculated.

"But why is he taking so long, then?" Ettie wondered aloud.

"He's probably in the back searching through thousands of layaway files," Elsa-May said.

"Not everyone buys things on layaway." Ettie was distracted by a sliver of light emanating from a partly open door at the end of the hallway. The light seemed to beckon, a soft glow against the encroaching darkness of the store. Compelled by curiosity, they both edged toward the door. Together, they pushed the door open fully and stepped into the dimly lit back room.

Instantly, a ghastly sight halted them in their tracks.

There, in the stark minimalism of the unlit room, lay Don Friesen. His body was splayed on the cold floor, eyes shut as though in a peaceful slumber that belied the grim reality. His skin was unnaturally pale, the stillness around him not of sleep but of an eternal rest, disturbed only by the stark reality of a large knife lodged firmly in his back.

Don Friesen was unmistakably dead!

Ettie and Elsa-May stood frozen to the spot as they tried to process the horrifying sight.

CHAPTER 3

*E*lsa-May inched closer to the body, her heart pounding as she grasped the gravity of their find. "Is he...?"

Ettie nodded solemnly as she bent down to check for any signs of life. After a moment, she straightened, her expression grim. "Yes, he's gone. Absolutely no doubt about it."

"We should call for help," Elsa-May murmured.

Ettie's eyes then caught sight of the ornate dagger coated in blood. She pointed at it, her voice steady despite the shock. "He didn't just die. He was murdered."

With a deep breath to steady her nerves, Elsa-May took a step back as Ettie moved out of the room, reached for the phone and dialed 911. She relayed their location and the nature of their discovery to the dispatcher who insisted that she remain on the line until the police arrived. But as a sudden noise echoed through the room, Ettie's survival instincts kicked in, and she abruptly ended the call.

Elsa-May leaned in, her voice tinged with fear. "Ettie, do you think the killer might still be nearby?"

Pausing, Ettie scanning the dimly lit corners of the room. "I heard something too, but it's hard to tell where it came from. There's no real place to hide in here."

Worry lined Elsa-May's face as she considered their vulnerable position. "Do you think Detective Kelly will be the one to come out and investigate this?"

"Maybe." Ettie chewed on her lip, her mind racing.

"Doesn't that man ever take a break?" Elsa-May half-joked, attempting to lighten the heaviness.

Ettie gave a half-hearted shrug. "I honestly don't know. But right now, we need him here. And soon."

As the silence stretched out, filling the room with its ominous presence, the sisters exchanged a look of mutual concern.

"But what about the key, the symbols, and the riddle?" Elsa-May's voice trembled.

"Forget about all that. None of it matters now," Ettie snapped.

"Oh, Ettie, he was killed. We could've passed the murderer on the street today. What if we'd come a few minutes earlier? We'd be dead too—killed." Elsa-May's voice cracked under the strain, her thoughts spiraling into a vortex of what-ifs. Tears pooled in her eyes, spilling over as she started sobbing.

In an impulse to snap her sister out of the spiral, Ettie reached out and slapped Elsa-May's face. The sound of the slap echoed sharply in the room.

Elsa-May drew in a sharp breath and stared at Ettie, her hand instinctively touching her stinging cheek. "What was that for?"

"You were getting hysterical. I read somewhere that's what you have to do. It worked, didn't it?"

Elsa-May's other hand now covered her cheek, cooling the burn. "That wasn't nice. How could you?"

"It worked," Ettie repeated.

Elsa-May nodded slowly, the initial shock fading slightly as she processed her sister's apology. "Let's just sit for a while." She moved to the nearest chair, her movements slow, as if the emotional weight she carried was a physical burden.

They both sat in silence, the only sound the relentless ticking of numerous clocks. After a moment, Ettie spoke again. "We can't let fear cloud our judgment. Don's death, this mystery with the key and the symbols... We need to figure this out, not just for Don, but for us too. We can't live looking over our shoulders."

Elsa-May looked at her sister. "All this just because you were bored. Next time, I'll ignore you and I won't go anywhere with you especially if you're going to slap me."

"Don wasn't killed because I was bored. I don't know what you're talking about. I'm sorry for slapping you. I panicked because you panicked. We need to stay calm. Especially with you and your high blood pressure."

"Well, forgive me. It's not as though I had a choice about that." Elsa-May's mouth turned down at the corners. "When I woke up today, I never thought we'd be doing this. I was looking forward to a quiet day of knitting."

Ettie rolled her eyes. *"Jah,* like every other day."

For the next few minutes, they sat in silence amid the ticking of multiple antique clocks.

Ettie picked up the binoculars and started looking at everything through them. Then without warning, the local police burst through the door. Ettie pushed herself to her feet and directed them to the backroom.

When Ettie came back to Elsa-May, Detective Kelly walked into the shop. His face was stern, his eyes scanning the room quickly before landing back on Ettie and Elsa-May, who were now standing up.

"You two never cease to amaze me," Kelly said as he approached.

"Thank you," Elsa-May said earning a dig in the ribs from Ettie.

"He doesn't mean it in a good way," Ettie whispered.

"Good morning, Detective Kelly." Just as Elsa-May

spoke, all the clocks chimed twelve times, signaling it was midday.

"She means good afternoon," Ettie said.

Elsa-May frowned at Ettie. "It was morning when I said it."

"You called about a dead man, possibly a murder victim?" Kelly asked.

Ettie responded, "We found Mr. Friesen in the back room. We... we do think he has been murdered. There was a large knife in his back."

"It was a dagger, Ettie, a fancy one."

Detective Kelly's eyes narrowed. "Did you know the victim?" Kelly asked.

"Yes. He is... he was Don Friesen."

"Gideon Friesen," Elsa-May corrected her sister. "We don't know much about him except that he owned this shop and he used to be Mennonite."

"Stay here." Detective Kelly left them and headed to the backroom. Ettie and Elsa-May followed and hovered in the doorway.

Ettie whispered to Elsa-May, "Let's keep the part about the key a secret, okay?"

"I think that's best. We don't want to confuse matters."

Detective Kelly crouched down, inspecting the body and the surroundings without touching a thing. After a moment, he straightened up and turned to one of the officers who had arrived before him. "Get the coroner and the forensics team down here right now."

"They're on the way, sir."

"And seal off this area; no one comes in." His voice was calm but authoritative.

The officer gave a nod and then left, speaking into his two-way radio.

Kelly then turned back to Ettie and Elsa-May and ushered them to the front of the store where they sat once more in the purple chairs while he stood, looming over them. "I need to know everything that happened. Start from the beginning, and don't leave out anything no matter how insignificant it may seem."

Ettie looked at Elsa-May wondering how much they should say.

Elsa-May began, "Well, it all started this morning. Ettie was depressed."

"I wouldn't say that. I just said that I was a bit sad. Depressed is a strong word."

Elsa-May stared at Ettie. "I'm sure you said depressed."

"I'm sure I didn't, Elsa-May. I'd remember if I said depressed."

"So would I and you did."

Kelly shook his head at them. "Can we fast forward to where we talk about the victim? When and where did you meet him?"

Ettie looked up at the ceiling, trying to work out how to leave out the part about the key.

"We can't keep it a secret any longer. We'll have to tell him everything, Ettie," Elsa-May whispered.

"Tell me what?" Kelly's head tilted to one side as he leaned down toward them.

CHAPTER 4

*E*ttie huffed at her sister. "Well, he came to us this morning at our home about a key that the baker next door found. It had strange symbols on it and he came to us because someone told him we were good at solving mysteries. That's what he'd been told."

"Wait a minute. That was just this morning?" Kelly asked.

"Yes, Detective." Ettie nodded.

Elsa-May gasped. "It just occurred to me. Do you think his murder has anything to do with the key?"

"We don't know anything right now, but I doubt it. You said the baker came across the key?"

Ettie nodded. "Yes, but he was worried about it."

"And it was old and Don liked old things."

Kelly took a notepad and pen out of his inner coat pocket. After he let out a long breath, he said, "You'd better tell me about this key then so I have a total picture of his final hours."

"We were next door looking at the key before we found him. The baker, Mrs. Henderson, is the keeper of the key. Then we came here to ask if he knew about the symbols inscribed on the key because Ettie saw them through a magnifying glass." Elsa-May pulled out the bit of paper with the scribbled symbols. "Look at this poem. Mrs. Henderson found it along with the key."

"At the same time," Ettie said. "She found the key in a loaf of bread. It was put there deliberately."

Kelly took it from her and then put it in his pocket. "I'll hang on to this. I don't think it's anything important since it was clearly for the baker, and too late for fingerprints now even if it was." Kelly pressed his lips together. "I'll talk to the baker as well and get her take on this."

"It's Mrs. Henderson," Ettie chirped.

"From next door," Elsa-May added.

"Both of you stay right here." He pointed at each of them in turn. "Don't go anywhere and don't touch anything—not one thing." He headed out the door as two officers wrapped the outside of the store in yellow crime scene tape.

Ettie shook her head at her sister.

"What now, Ettie? You've got that disapproving scowl on your face."

"You made it sound like I wanted to keep something from him when you said we'd *have to tell him now*."

"You *did* want to keep it from him."

"Yes, but I didn't want him to know it."

"I couldn't lie," Elsa-May stated with a slight shoulder shrug.

"I can't believe you said Mrs. Henderson was 'the keeper of the key.'"

"She is!"

"It sounds so weird when you said that—the keeper of the key. Like the mystery is so much bigger than it is. It's just an old key in a loaf of bread and now we're stuck in a crime scene," Ettie said.

"Poor old Don." Elsa-May hung her head.

"I know. I wonder who could've killed him. Hopefully, they'll find out soon." Ettie looked around. "Maybe they were stealing something, and he tried to stop them." She recalled the cabinet full of precious items and stood up and wandered over to it.

"Hey, Detective Kelly said not to move. Whenever you do something stupid he blames us both."

Ettie ignored her sister and kept looking at the sparkly objects. "I wonder if all this is real. If it is, then I think we can rule out robbery with all of this still here."

"Ettie, just sit back down. I don't like it when Detective Kelly gets angry with us. I hope you haven't caused trouble for Mrs. Henderson now."

"Me?" Ettie's eyes bugged open and she pointed at herself.

"Yes, you!"

"Oh dear. I wouldn't want to do that deliberately." Ettie did what her sister said and sat down beside her. "Why did you tell the detective I was depressed? That's embarrassing like I'm some tragic depressed old lady."

Elsa-May looked away from Ettie.

"I'm not like that!" Ettie insisted.

"If you say so. Anyway, Kelly said to start at the beginning and that was the beginning of our day. And before you start getting angry with me about the key, we had to tell him about that. How could we not? That's the reason we're here."

"I know we had to tell him in the end, but you didn't have to add the extra bits."

"I suppose you're right. I'm sorry you were depressed, sad, or whatever mood you were you in."

Ettie knew it was no use saying anything to her sister.

"What's the matter now, Ettie? I apologized and you're still not happy."

"You should apologize for saying what you said, not apologizing for me being in a funny mood this morning."

"Funny? There was nothing funny about you this morning."

Ettie grunted. "Let's just sit in silence, shall we?"

"Gladly. It'll be more enjoyable that way."

While waiting for Kelly, the gloom over the antique shop seemed to grow even heavier. The ticking clocks seemed to echo louder, as if counting down the seconds to the next unforeseen event.

Kelly's expression was unreadable when he returned, the doorbell chiming softly as he entered.

CHAPTER 5

"*I* spoke with Mrs. Henderson," Kelly began. "She corroborated your story about the key, and she's understandably upset. She didn't take the news about the murder well at all. I had to call the paramedics. She kept saying that she didn't know a key could lead to his murder."

"That's odd that she'd think her key would be connected to Don's murder." Ettie studied the Detective's face trying to read what he was thinking.

Elsa-May wrung her hands. "Do you think there's a connection now, Detective? Between the key and the man's death?"

"And the poem," Ettie said. "Don't forget the poem. What was the poem again, Elsa-May?"

"I don't remember. It was taken from me."

"That's something we'll have to look into, Mrs. Smith," Kelly replied. "Right now, every piece of information is a potential part of the puzzle. This key and the note could all be related, or it could be an unfortunate coincidence. But in my line of work, I've learned that coincidences are not as common as people think."

Ettie leaned forward, her eyes searching Kelly's. "What happens now, Detective?"

"Now," Kelly sighed, glancing back toward the room where Don lay, "we'll conduct a thorough investigation. We'll start with everything about the cause of death. The coroner's report will tell us what we need to know."

Ettie and Elsa-May looked at each other. "Well, he did have a knife in his back."

Kelly nodded. "But there are many nuances to do with stabbing. Blood spatter and such. And then there is the weapon itself."

Ettie peered into Kelly's face. "You look pale and tired."

"I'm not getting much sleep, but that comes with the job. We'll also look into the victim's background. Check if he had any enemies, debts, or recent strange occurrences in his life—all the usual things."

"And what about us?" Elsa-May asked.

Kelly's gaze softened. "I want you both to go home, relax, and write down everything you remember from today, every little detail. Then come and see me tomorrow and we'll go over everything."

"But we're involved now, aren't we? Because we

talked to Don about the key. What if whoever did this comes after us?"

Elsa-May nodded. "And what if we past the killer in the street while walking from the bakery to here? We might have. He might think we saw him, and he doesn't know we didn't know who he was. He could try to silence us so we can't identify him."

"Don't jump to conclusions. To ease your mind, I'll have patrol cars drive past your home every now and again for the next day or so. Okay, happy?"

The sisters exchanged glances, each thinking that wasn't much by way of protection. "Can't you have someone stay in a car outside our home?" Ettie asked.

Kelly shook his head. "I'm sorry. We're short staffed."

"Can we go home now?" Elsa-May inquired.

"In a moment," Kelly responded. "I just want to say one more thing. Leave this to us. It's dangerous to pursue leads on your own. This has nothing to do with your Amish community so I will not be using your help this time."

Elsa-May looked over at Ettie who nodded, and then said, "We'll see you tomorrow."

"I'll have someone drive you home." Kelly frowned at Ettie as his gaze dropped to the binoculars. "Interesting necklace."

"Oh these? They're my new bird watching binoculars. Elsa-May, would you go back there and find somewhere to leave twenty dollars?"

"I suppose you want me to pay for them too?" Elsa-May inquired.

"Of course."

Elsa-May gave Ettie a nod and went to the counter and found a money tin and placed twenty dollars inside.

As they were escorted to the police vehicle for a ride home, Ettie glanced back at the antique shop, now marked with the garish yellow crime scene tape. Would the mysteries locked within those old walls ever see the light of day?

CHAPTER 6

The next day, Ettie and Elsa-May approached the police station with a sense of urgency in their steps. The morning air was brisk, and their breaths materialized in tiny puffs of fog.

The station was its usual buzz of activity, but everything seemed more intense, more urgent somehow. A uniformed officer quickly ushered them into Detective Kelly's small office, where he stood waiting, looking weary.

After they greeted one another, Ettie was the first to speak. "We've been thinking hard about yesterday, about everything Mr. Friesen might have said or done that seemed... odd."

Elsa-May chimed in, "Yes, we remembered he might have looked over his shoulder as if he was worried about being watched."

SAMANTHA PRICE

Kelly nodded, jotting down notes. "Hmm, might have. Anything specific he said that stood out to you?"

The sisters shared a glance, delving into their memories of their brief conversations with Don. "Not really."

Elsa-May added, "He seemed quite preoccupied with getting back to his store while we were looking at the key."

"Why did he come to you if you'd never met him before?" Kelly asked.

Memories clicked into place, and Ettie's eyes widened. "Oh, he did mention Ava to us. She was the one who told him to come to us about the key."

"Ava?"

Ettie's brow furrowed. "Yes. She's married to my great nephew, Jeremiah. He is also Elsa-May's grand-son. She's a regular customer of the antique store, Don told us."

"I remember Ava. I met her years ago when she was helping the pair of you with something or other. Has she always been in your community?" Kelly picked up a folder and started flipping through notes.

"She left for a time. She returned to the community a while back and had been living in the house I inherited from my dear friend, Agatha," Ettie explained.

Elsa-May leaned forward. "That was before Ava married my grandson. She's become a dear part of our family and they have two delightful sons now. But why do you ask, Detective?"

42

Kelly was quiet for a moment, reading something and then he looked up. "Did you know Ava once worked for Don Friesen?" Kelly asked them.

The sisters exchanged shocked glances. "Worked for him?" Elsa-May echoed in disbelief.

"Yes. We found it in his records, and her name was also recorded in his books as his last sale before...well, before he died. She bought a copper jug from him the day before yesterday. I have a copy of the receipt here." The detective observed them carefully. "Is it possible she's involved in something deeper here? Could there be a reason she bought that jug, or a reason she was the last person who purchased an item from him?"

Elsa-May bristled. "Absolutely not. She wouldn't hurt a fly, and besides that, what could possibly be suspicious about buying a jug?"

Kelly held up his hands. "I'm not accusing her of anything. But it's a lead we can't ignore. I need to talk with her, understand the nature of their transaction, their relationship."

Ettie felt a knot of worry form in her stomach. "She's not a suspect, is she?"

The detective shrugged slightly. "At this stage, we keep all options open. But what do you think?"

Both sisters were vehement in shaking their heads. "No, she's not capable of any wrongdoing," Elsa-May said with conviction.

Kelly nodded, his expression softening. "I understand your concerns. I'll ensure the conversation is just a casual chat for now. What else can you tell me?"

"Nothing more than we told you yesterday," Ettie said.

"Well, let's go over it one more time starting at the beginning. From when the victim knocked on your door to when you found him in the backroom of his shop."

The sisters repeated it all again and when they were done, Ettie asked him what he'd found out so far.

"You know I can't tell you that, but I can tell you we don't have much at this stage of the investigation. We'll need to find out everything we can about him. Was he involved in shady deals, did anyone owe him money, did he owe money, or did he have links to anything involving crime?"

"I do recall that Mrs. Henderson said there was a suspicious stranger in her shop the other day."

"I'm talking with her again today. There's a long road ahead of us."

"We best not keep you then," Elsa-May said as she stood up.

Kelly frowned. "Come back tomorrow. Think hard. Both of you are key witnesses seeing you saw him so soon before his death."

Elsa-May stifled a laugh.

Kelly frowned at her. "What do you find funny?"

"You said 'key' witnesses. I'm thinking about the key that was found and now we are key witnesses."

Ettie looked down. Her sister was getting on the wrong side of Kelly and that wouldn't end well.

Kelly's face remained stony. "I'll see you tomorrow then." He got up and walked them out of the station.

CHAPTER 7

*A*s the sisters walked along the pavement away from the police station, Elsa-May chuckled again. "We are key witnesses. Get it, Ettie, key?"

"You shouldn't have laughed about that. You know Detective Kelly has no sense of humor."

"I couldn't resist it."

"Let's just concentrate on getting to Ava's house. We need to warn her Kelly's coming to see her."

Elsa-May stepped out onto the road and waved down a taxi.

Several minutes later, the taxi's wheels crunched over the gravel of Ava's driveway. The sisters paid the fare and hastened to the front door.

After their knuckles rapped against the wood, the door opened to reveal a surprised Ava. "Hello. Is everything okay?"

Elsa-May spoke first. "We need to talk. May we come in?"

"Of course." With a nod, Ava stepped aside, allowing the sisters to come in. They settled on the couches in the living room.

Ettie took a deep breath, her voice steady despite the tremor she felt. "Ava, dear, there's been a... a terrible incident."

Elsa-May picked up where Ettie faltered, "Don Friesen, the antique dealer, he's... he's passed away. He was found in his shop."

A gasp escaped Ava, her hand flying to her mouth as her eyes brimmed with disbelief. "That's awful."

"There's more. He didn't just die of natural causes. He was murdered," Ettie said.

Ava covered her mouth with her hand. "No. Oh, that's awful. Who did it?"

Elsa-May shook her head. "No one knows yet."

"I saw him just a couple of days ago. Did he come to see you? I told him about the two of you. He was worried about some key that the baker found in a loaf of bread."

"He came to see us yesterday, and he died that same afternoon."

Ava hung her head. "I'm sorry I mentioned you now. The baker next door to him was particularly worried about the key and that's what was concerning Don."

Ettie continued, "There's more. Detective Kelly told

us you were one of the last people to interact with Don. You bought a jug from him, remember?"

Ava's complexion paled, her confusion morphing into concern. "Yes, I was there the other day. I bought a copper jug. It's in the kitchen. I was just cleaning it up now. I'll be using it for a water jug."

Elsa-May patted her hand reassuringly. "Detective Kelly is going to ask you questions. He knows about your past employment with Don and about the purchase. He might come to talk with you."

"Am I in trouble or something? Does he think I killed him?"

Ettie shook her head. "No. Nothing like that. We just wanted to warn you, prepare you so you didn't get a shock when he knocked on your door."

The atmosphere was heavy with concern as Ava absorbed the information shared by the sisters. "He was always fascinated by keys," she murmured, almost to herself, a memory sparking in her eyes.

Ettie exchanged a look with Elsa-May before turning her attention back to Ava. "What are you thinking, Ava?"

"Years ago, when I was working at Don's store, he showed me a unique old key. He was peculiar about it, said it was 'a key with no door yet discovered.' He loved his mysteries," she said with a half-smile that quickly faded. "He didn't sell it, claimed he needed to know its story first."

"Do you believe it's the same key found in

the bread?" Elsa-May asked, the lines on her forehead deepening.

Ettie frowned. "No, of course not. He would've recognized it. It must be a different key. And it also came with a poem."

Ava's head tilted to one side. "What was the poem?"

"Just a confusing jumble of nonsense. I did have it, but Detective Kelly took it from me."

"Well, maybe the poem that Mrs. Henderson found had nothing to do with the key, but it's just weird that she found the poem on the same day and the poem mentions the key. And then he ends up dead!" Ettie added.

Elsa-May's mind raced. "Ava, did Don have any enemies?"

"I don't know," Ava confessed, her hands clasped tightly. "But Don was friendly, often sharing stories of his antiques with customers. Maybe he revealed too much to the wrong person. Or he might've exaggerated something, and someone believed one of his stories."

The room was silent as they all considered the dangerous implications. "We're now in the middle of this, whether we like it or not. It's a riddle for certain. Why did the key end up in the bread?" Elsa-May inquired.

"Perhaps someone was trying to hide it," Ettie suggested.

They heard a car pull up outside and Ava stood to look out the window. "It's the detective. He's here."

CHAPTER 8

*E*lsa-May sprang to her feet. "Oh, Ettie, he shouldn't see us here."

"You can go out the back, wait in the barn and I'll drive you home," Ava suggested.

"Let's go, Elsa-May." Ettie reached over, patting Ava's hand. "Speak with the detective, but only facts, no assumptions. We don't want suspicion pointed your way."

Ava nodded. "I don't have anything to hide."

As the sisters slipped out the back door, the brisk air met them with an urgency that matched the rapid pounding in their chests.

Inside the barn, the familiar earthy scent of hay and the soft snuffling of the resident animals were oddly comforting under the circumstances. They settled into a hidden corner, obscured by stacks of hay bales.

Elsa-May drew a deep breath. "Ettie, the key is more important than we thought."

"If that's so, why wasn't Mrs. Henderson killed? She's the one with the key."

"I'm not sure. Maybe the killer thought Don had it. I'm just worried about our safety now. I hope Mrs. Henderson will be all right too."

Ettie lowered her head. "But it's not in our hands, Elsa-May. The baker has the key so that at least means we're not immediate targets."

"Not unless the killer thinks we saw him leaving the antique shop. But another thing I've been thinking. When Don was talking to us it sounded like he barely knew Ava. Why was that?"

"You're right, Ettie. He was even calling her a different name. He could've said a woman who used to work for him, but instead he said she was a customer. I guess she was a customer as well."

Ettie nodded. "What if he was losing his mind?"

"It's possible. Or maybe he didn't want to involve her too much."

A few minutes later, they heard the car leaving. Ettie opened the door a little and used her binoculars. "He's gone, Elsa-May. Hey, these are coming in handy."

"He didn't stay long. Come on, Ettie."

They walked out of the barn and saw Ava walking toward them.

"What did he say?" Elsa-May asked.

"He just asked about my impressions when I shopped there and used to work there, and how well I knew Don. Whether he was married or not and some other personal questions about him."

"He told us he wasn't married," Ettie asked.

"He was at one point. I'm pretty sure I overheard him tell someone that he never divorced, so that would mean that technically he's still married, and I guess that if he hasn't left a will, his wife would inherit all he had."

Elsa-May raised her eyebrows. "Interesting. And where was he living?"

"Above the store. Let me tell you about Don's wife."

"Go on," Elsa-May said.

"She was a tough woman. They must've separated just before I started working there. She would come into the shop and just walk out with things."

"Why would she do that?" Elsa-May asked.

"She said the business was half hers. I didn't know if that was true or not so I couldn't stop her. Don said to just let her go. After a while she stopped coming in."

"You said he lived above the store?" Elsa-May asked.

"Well, he might not live there now, but when I worked there, he always lived above the store. Before that, he lived in a house with his wife and her son from a previous marriage. What do we do now? I want to help," Ava said.

"Oh no, Ava. You can't do anything. We'll get into trouble with Jeremiah."

Ettie nodded. "You know how Jeremiah doesn't like you to involve yourself in anything."

"I'm already involved. I'll drive you both home and then I'll need to be back for when the boys get home from school."

Several minutes later, the sound of the buggy wheels rolling over the compacted earth was a comforting, calming rhythm and helped soothe Ettie's jangled nerves. Sitting in the backseat behind Elsa-May and away from her older sister's judgement, Ettie looked at everything through her 'field glasses.'

"I wonder if he was killed over the key and now isn't Mrs. Henderson in danger if she still has that key?" Ava asked.

Elsa-May cast her gaze toward the open fields. "What if the killer thinks *we* have the key? That's what I'm worried about. It's like the peace of our days has been disturbed."

"Maybe his death was nothing to do with the key," Ettie said as she placed her binoculars in her lap.

"Perhaps it wasn't an intentional murder. The man could've been trying to rob the place and then he panicked. Or it could've been someone settling a score," Ava suggested.

Elsa-May let out a loud sigh. "Whatever it was, I feel so sorry for Don's last moments."

When the sisters finally got to their house, they got

out of the horse and buggy slowly. After their goodbyes were said, they watched Ava drive away.

Sitting in their living room, the sisters felt the weight of the day's revelations.

"What about if Don knew more about the key than he was letting on?"

Elsa-May shook her head. "No. Why would he involve us if he knew anything?"

"Hmm. That's the thing then, isn't it? Why would he come here, as if it's some big thing? It was just a key. Why was he so troubled by it?" Ettie tapped her chin as she thought some more. "Elsa-May, the antique store is a crime scene, but what about his home? Ava said he lived above his store. What if we take a look around and see what we can see?"

CHAPTER 9

*E*lsa-May stared at her sister, while contemplating her suggestion. "You mean you want to break-in to Don's home?"

"No, I mean just take a look around."

"You know that's the same thing. Anyway, how would we get in? It's not as though we have a..."

"A key?" Ettie finished her sister's sentence.

"That's right. I hesitated to say that word given the circumstances."

"I don't have all the answers. We need to know more about him. Did he have debts, was he sent threatening letters? And we need to do that before someone clears out all his stuff and throws it away. That's what they do with dead people's things."

Elsa-May sighed deeply, her fingers tracing the wood grain of her chair's armrest. "Yes, his relatives might clear things out, but breaking in... Ettie, that's against our way."

Ettie leaned forward. "I know, Elsa-May, I know. But think about it, we're not doing harm. We're seeking truth, for Don's sake. He came to us, and we gave our word we'd help. Just because he's dead doesn't mean we take back what we said. Think of it like this, him asking us for our help was also giving us permission to look around his home."

"That's a stretch even for your vivid imagination."

Ettie wasn't listening. "We might find a spare key hidden under the front door mat or in a nearby pot plant."

Elsa-May's expression softened. "Alright, Ettie. I know that if I don't agree, you'd only go by yourself and get into trouble. You can enter respectfully and take a look around while I wait outside."

"Good thinking. You can keep a lookout."

Elsa-May frowned. "I don't like the sound of that."

"Good! So we'll go after dusk, when the streets will be empty, to avoid drawing attention."

"How do I get into these things?" Elsa-May asked.

Hours later, the two sisters were walking down to the shanty to call a taxi. Elsa-May gave Ettie a sidelong glance, noticing her field glasses. "Why do you still have those on?"

Ettie looked down and lifted her binoculars. "These? I might spot a bird."

"What? An owl?"

"You never know. I'm getting quite used to them. You never know when they'll be useful for things and not just bird watching."

Elsa-May huffed. "If you think so, Ettie."

"I do."

Half an hour and one taxi ride later, the antique store, silent and dark, loomed above them as they approached. They found a door on the side of the building that led up to Don's living quarters.

After climbing the stairs, they stood at his door. The only light was the glow coming in from the streetlight outside. Elsa-May switched on a small flashlight she'd brought with her. "There's no pot plant and no doormat to hide a key. What now, genius?"

Ettie reached up her hand and on the ledge above the door, she retrieved a key. She grinned as she held it in front of Elsa-May's face. "What's this? Oh, it's a key." Ettie chuckled.

"All right, all right. Just see if it opens the door. If it doesn't you won't be so happy."

Ettie slid the key into the lock and turned it, hearing the satisfying click of the tumblers falling into place. As she swung the door open, Elsa-May, swept up in the excitement, momentarily forgot her earlier resolve not to enter. With a rush of curiosity, she hurried after Ettie, stepping quickly through the doorway right behind her.

The living space was modest, cluttered with various antiques and personal effects. Papers were strewn across his desk, and the remnants of his last day were hauntingly present—an empty coffee cup sat beside an open book.

They split up to cover more ground. Elsa-May examined the desk, rifling through the papers for any sign of debt or threats. Ettie searched the shelves, looking behind books and trinkets. Once Elsa-May was done she went to the small kitchen, opening drawers and cupboards.

Elsa-May's fingers stumbled upon a series of letters tucked away in a drawer. They were notices of overdue payments, and a couple of them were indeed threatening in tone. "Ettie, look at this."

Ettie rushed into the kitchen and looked over Elsa-May's shoulder. "Debts...he had debts," she murmured. "But would that be a motive for murder? The amounts aren't large. Maybe he simply forgot to pay them."

"It's a start," Elsa-May replied, her mind racing. "I guess the police thought this wasn't important. They were right here in plain sight and they must've searched his house by now. Let's keep looking."

As soon as Ettie was back in the living area, she spied a small box on the top of one of the bookcases. She reached up and grabbed it. "I found a box," she announced, bringing the box to the table. With a shaky hand, Ettie opened the lid.

Inside the box were several items: a photograph of Don when he was younger with an unknown woman and child, and a small stack of cash.

"Put it back, Ettie. We'll leave this for the police to find when they get around to it. It could be his ex wife and maybe their child."

"Current wife because Ava said they're still legally married."

"Well, they could be the current family then."

"I suppose this doesn't tell us anything." Ettie gently closed the lid and put it back where she found it.

"Well, I think we've done all we can." Elsa-May put her hands on her hips and turned around. Then she spotted a small piece of paper on the floor. She leaned down to pick it up and saw there was nothing written on it.

Intending to dispose of it, she headed to the kitchen where she'd seen a waste bin. Once she lifted the lid, the sight caught her off guard. It was filled with an assortment of pastries, scones, eclairs, and cream-filled delights. "Ettie, come look at this."

Ettie approached, peering into the bin as Elsa-May held up the paper, now forgotten in her hand. "Why would Don have all these cakes in here?"

"Maybe it was leftovers from the bakery."

"Maybe, but I'm sure Mrs. Henderson has her own waste disposal."

"It's a shame. I hate to see things go to waste. They look like they haven't even been touched. Oh, that cream looks delicious." Elsa-May reached out.

"Stop. Don't do that, Elsa-May. They would be off by now."

"I was just going to touch them."

"Could someone have brought those cakes to him as a gift or... perhaps as a peace offering?" Ettie speculated, her mind racing through scenarios.

"Well, without finding a note, it would be hard to say. Dead people can't tell us anything."

"Not unless we can find a clue, then they're telling us something. There's nothing here that tells us anything, though," Ettie said having a last look around.

"Well, perhaps that does tell us something."

Ettie frowned at her sister. "Are you trying to be funny?"

"No. All we found are some stale cakes and nothing else. Maybe it was just a random killing and a robbery gone wrong like Ava said."

"You might be right for once."

Elsa-May's eyebrows rose. "For once?"

"Let's just go home."

"Gladly," Elsa-May said heading for the door. "I didn't want to come here in the first place."

CHAPTER 10

The following day, Ettie and Elsa-May decided they should speak with Mrs. Henderson again to see if she might have some insight into who killed Don.

As they approached the bakery, they noticed a figure busily working at the door of the antique store next door. It was a man they hadn't seen before, focused intently on installing a new lock. Tools were scattered at his feet, and he hummed a melody.

Ettie exchanged a curious glance with her sister before approaching. "Good morning, sir. That's quite a job you're doing there."

The man looked up, wiping his brow with the back of his hand. "Ah, yes. The police needed the store secured. Couldn't find the key, they said. Entire place is a crime scene now."

Elsa-May adjusted her shawl, a chill running down her spine. "It's so tragic what happened to Mr. Friesen."

The locksmith clicked the new lock into place and gathered his tools, not meeting their eyes. "Tragic, yes, but not surprising, if you ask me."

The sisters shared a puzzled look. "Not surprising?" Ettie echoed.

He finally looked up, his expression somber. "Mr. Friesen ruffled a lot of feathers in his time. In this business, you hear things."

"Enemies?" Elsa-May's voice was a mere whisper.

"Yeah, lots of disputes with other dealers, competitors, disgruntled customers... you name it. But there was one who always seemed to be at odds with him." He hesitated, as if considering whether to continue. "An antique dealer by the name of Joy Basket. She has a store two blocks up. There were rumors that they were always undercutting each other's deals, always bumping heads."

Ettie clasped her hands in front of her, the name registering. "Joy Basket, you say?"

"That's right."

"You knew the old man?"

"We were recent acquaintances."

Ettie and Elsa-May read each other's thoughts. They turned and walked in the direction of Joy Basket's store.

The streets were quieter, the town still reeling from the shock of losing a prominent member. With each step, Ettie and Elsa-May prepared themselves to meet Joy, unsure of what they might uncover.

The sign for "Basket's Antiques" came into view, a quaint storefront that gave off an aura of history and countless untold stories. The window display was an eclectic mix of items, from ornate lamps to porcelain dolls, each likely possessing its unique past. They paused at the entrance, collecting their thoughts before entering.

The bell above the door announced their arrival, and they were greeted by a world of relics. The musty scent of old books blended with the dried flower arrangements, and every surface was adorned with artifacts and trinkets. It was just like stepping into Don's antique store minus the floral arrangements.

Behind the counter stood a woman, presumably Joy Basket. She was in her mid-fifties, with sharp features and a scrutinizing gaze that softened slightly at the sight of the two elderly ladies.

"Welcome to Basket's Antiques. How may I assist you today?" Her voice had a formal quality, and she assessed the sisters with a curious tilt of her head.

Elsa-May took the lead. "Good day, Ms. Basket. We're here about Don Friesen. We understand you knew him."

At the mention of Don's name, a shadow passed over Joy's face, her professional facade wavering. "Yes, I knew Don. Heard about the terrible incident. It's a shock, truly." She paused, her fingers nervously adjusting a stray price tag. "How did you two know him?"

"We'd met him recently," Ettie explained.

"We met him on the very day he died," Elsa-May said.

"And he had a peculiar encounter concerning a key and some bread from Mrs. Henderson's bakery."

"Is that so?" Joy asked.

"Yes." Ettie said with a nod.

"Many peculiar stories floated around Don. He was certainly one for the dramatic even to the very last day it seems."

Elsa-May leaned in a bit closer, lowering her voice. "We heard that you and he had some professional rivalry."

Joy's expression hardened. "That was business. Yes, Don and I were competitors. He could be underhanded, always flaunting his latest 'treasures.' But I had no reason to wish him harm. It's all part of the game."

"We're merely trying to make sense of the mysterious key—it's all a bit unsettling," Ettie said.

Joy sighed, her stance relaxing. "Don may have been a thorn in my side, but our rivalry was nothing serious. It kept us sharp." She hesitated, then gestured to a small sitting area. "Why don't we sit? I can share what I know if you are truly interested in hearing a story."

Ettie's eyebrows rose. "We are."

Joy showed them into a small sitting area that had a sign 'Staff Only.'

As they settled into their seats, Joy seemed to readjust her demeanor, softening even further in the more comfortable setting. However, before she began her account, she held up a hand, a small smile pulling at the corners of her mouth. "Before we go any further, I feel I must correct a small detail," she interjected, her tone light despite the gravity of their discussion. "My last name often causes quite the confusion. It's pronounced 'Bask-kay,' rhymes with 'day.' Over the years, I've heard a range of mispronunciations, but I prefer to set the record straight the first time I meet anyone."

Ettie and Elsa-May exchanged a brief, amused glance, appreciating the interlude to the tension that had built up.

"Thank you, Ms. Bask-kay," Ettie responded with a respectful nod, emphasizing the correct pronunciation.

"It's Mrs not Ms. My husband died some years ago."

"Sorry to hear that. We appreciate the clarification."

Elsa-May felt the need to share, that they were just copying the name from how the locksmith said it.

"Not a problem at all," Joy replied, her smile lingering for a moment more before it faded, replaced by the serious expression she wore earlier. "Now, where were we? Ah, yes, my professional relationship with Don."

Joy Basket then recounted some business dealings she had with Don.

Mrs. Basket's eyes darted between Ettie and Elsa-

May. "And if you don't mind me asking, why are you so interested in all this?"

Ettie's mouth fell open in shock at the blunt question before she replied, "The police questioned a friend of ours about Don's death and we don't want her to be blamed for something she didn't do."

"I don't know who killed him, but I can tell you this much, Don had enemies. He meddled in people's lives, always looking for opportunities to exploit them. I won't shed a tear for him, but I had no hand in his demise. You're looking in the wrong place if you're trying to find out who snuffed out his lights. I did hear a rumor, though."

Elsa-May leaned forward. "About Don?"

"Yes. Well, it was more than a rumor, it was a fact. There was a land dispute between him and Cedric Zabrik."

"What kind of a dispute?" Elsa-May sat on the edge of her seat.

"This is going back a few years. Don bought land that he intended to develop. He couldn't go ahead when Cedric lodged an objection. It was something to do with a boundary line, I'm fairly certain. I can't give you any precise details, but that might give you another avenue to explore."

"And where could we find Cedric Zabrik?" Ettie asked.

Joy's lips twisted into a smile. "He runs the local post office. You can't miss him, he's as bald as a bowling ball and looks like one too. Oh, and don't say I said anything. You didn't hear it from me. And also, I must mention that Don and his wife have been separated for eons, with, so I'm told from the rumor mill, that there was no divorce in sight. So... wouldn't she inherit everything now? Her son didn't help matters between them."

"Her son?" Ettie inquired.

"Yes, hers because he wasn't Don's son. He was *her* son from a previous marriage I suppose."

"I see." Ettie tapped on her chin.

"Again, you didn't hear it from me." Joy gave them a wink.

CHAPTER 11

*E*ttie and Elsa-May thanked Mrs. Basket for her time and as they walked away, the sisters couldn't help but feel a twinge of suspicion.

"That was odd, Ettie, don't you think? Mrs. Basket was quick to push suspicion onto other people. That sparks some concern."

"No. I just think she's a little eccentric, and there's nothing wrong with that. I'd dare say she'd be a hard woman to get along with."

"Yes, and with an attitude like that, she could make a few enemies herself. Before we find Cedric Zabrik, let's head back and see Mrs. Henderson."

"No, Ettie. We forgot. We were supposed to see Detective Kelly again today."

"Oh. That's right."

They made their way to the police station and were

immediately escorted to Detective Kelly's office, where they were told he wouldn't be long.

After a minute, Ettie got bored. She stood up, circled around Kelly's desk, and plopped herself into his chair. She sank right in and her back was nicely cradled into a soft but firm support. "Oh, Elsa-May, you have to try this! It's like sitting on a cloud made of marshmallows."

"Get off there now. What do you think he'll say when he sees you?"

"I wouldn't worry about it." Ettie waved her hand dismissively and spotted an untouched coffee cup on the desk. "He's probably off saving the world or something. He'll be ages." She closed her eyes and sighed dramatically. "This is unbelievable. We need to get a chair like this for home. I could sit on it and watch the birds out the window."

Elsa-May couldn't resist any longer. "Alright, my turn!"

"No, just a bit longer."

"Hurry up!"

"Okay, okay." The sisters swapped places.

"You're right about something for once, Ettie. This is comfortable. And it swivels!" Elsa-May gave an exaggerated spin in the chair, doing a complete circle.

"Why don't you have a sip of his coffee? He won't want it now, and I know you like it cold."

Elsa-May gave her sister a mock stern look but then

picked up the coffee cup and held it to her lips just as Detective Kelly walked through the door.

"What's going on here?" His voice boomed across the room, freezing Elsa-May mid-sip. "Have you decided to take over my job now?"

"I'm dreadfully sorry!" Elsa-May quickly set the cup down and scrambled back to her seat next to Ettie, her face as red as a beet. "How could you do that to me, Ettie?" Elsa-May whispered.

"How would I know he'd walk in when he did?"

Elsa-May pressed her lips together. "I don't know, but I think you did."

After Detective Kelly sat down, he looked over at them. "Mrs. Smith, Mrs. Lutz, good morning. Thank you for coming in today. I have some news that might interest you."

Elsa-May noticed a neat stack of files pushed to one edge of his desk. "Did you speak with Ava?"

"Yes. She was very helpful."

"Good." Elsa-May gave a nod.

Detective Kelly leaned forward. "The bakery, Mrs. Henderson's place, was broken into last night. She reported it around 3 am when she arrived to start baking."

Elsa-May brought a hand to her chest. "Oh, my! Is she alright?"

"She's fine, just shaken. Nothing was stolen except..." He paused, then pulled the files closer to him. "Except for that old key she found."

Ettie and Elsa-May exchanged shocked looks. "That's terrible," Elsa-May said as she shook her head.

Detective Kelly eyed them carefully, reading their expressions. "I'm starting to think that this key might have something to do with Friesen's murder after all. I can't rule it out as a coincidence just yet. In hindsight we probably should've taken it into evidence."

"But what could possibly be so important about that old key?" Ettie wondered aloud.

"It must open something pretty special," Elsa-May said.

"But couldn't they open it with a hammer? I mean if it opened a special treasure box or something, if someone really wants what's inside, who needs a key?" Ettie inquired.

"That's what we need to find out." Kelly grabbed a pen and a notebook, and then looked up at the sisters. "I'm going to need a full account of your recent interactions with both the victim and Mrs. Henderson. Also, any other unusual occurrences you can recall might be useful."

Ettie shrugged. "We don't know much, just what we already told you."

"Think hard. Did you notice anything unusual when you got to Don's antique store?" Kelly asked them.

"No. Just that he had a lot of stuff. Too much stuff and we could hardly walk because there were things everywhere. And oh, those clocks going off at the one time. It was a lot for my head."

Kelly frowned and then looked over at Ettie. "Mrs. Smith?"

Ettie looked up at the ceiling as she thought. "Those purple chairs were quite comfortable too, weren't they, Elsa-May?"

Elsa-May blushed again, thinking about how she was caught in the detective's chair just now. "Yes. They were."

"Ladies, please try to remember something. You've had a day to think some more about it. Any small detail might be crucial, a piece of a puzzle that we could need."

Ettie thought back. "We entered the store and saw things piled up everywhere. We were surprised by the clutter. Well, I was, and then we saw a door open."

"And heard all the clocks ticking. Tic toc, tic toc. I'm glad we don't have a loud ticking clock at home, it would drive me mad."

"Apart from the junk and the ticking clocks, anything else? And please don't mention clutter or clocks again."

"That's about it. Detective Kelly, do you think Don had enemies?" Ettie asked. "I mean we know he had one because he was killed. I'm sorry, that was a silly question."

"Enemies?" he repeated, placing his pen down and giving her his full attention.

Ettie, feeling a bit self-conscious under his gaze, continued, "Yes, we heard that Don might have had disputes with other people in his line of work. In fact, there's another antique dealer, Joy Basket—her name is pronounced 'Bask-kay,'" she corrected herself quickly, remembering the emphasis. "She seemed to have a rather competitive relationship with Don."

Elsa-May chimed in, "Yes, we spoke with her earlier today. She implied that their rivalry was just business, but it seemed like there was more to it, at least from her side."

Detective Kelly's expression shifted, a glint of interest behind his eyes. He leaned back in his chair, considering the information. "Joy Basket," he murmured, as if testing the name on his tongue. "I'm familiar with her and her store. My wife, before she left me and filed for divorce, bought a lamp from her. I know because she decided she didn't like it after we had it for a week, and she had me take it back for a refund."

Elsa-May pursed her lips. "Did Joy give you a refund?"

"No, but she let me choose something else. That's not important though."

Now Ettie had to know. "What did you choose?"

Kelly hung his head. "Something that the wife didn't like so she had me take it back again. It was all a huge debacle. After a few times, I had to pretend Joy Basket gave us a refund and handed the money to my wife."

"We're so sorry," Elsa-May said.

Kelly nodded. "Thanks, it was an inconvenience to keep going there. I don't like shopping at the best of times."

"Elsa-May means she's sorry about the divorce. Isn't that right, Elsa-May?"

"That's correct."

"Oh, thank you. Me too, but what can you do? This job is not easy for a spouse to deal with. Already being familiar with Joy Basket might be an advantage. So, the lamp debacle wasn't all for nothing."

"We told her we were there because a friend of ours was a friend of Don's," Ettie said.

The detective seemed to mull over a thought privately before continuing. "In this town, relationships, especially business ones, can be more complicated than they appear on the surface. Perhaps Mrs. Basket knows something more than she told you."

Ettie pressed her lips together, contemplating. "She spoke of Don in past tense, with a sort of... finality. It was subtle, but it felt like there was an undercurrent of relief, maybe even a hint of bitterness."

"Why wouldn't she talk about him in a final way, Ettie? He's dead. He's not coming back."

Detective Kelly nodded, jotting down something in his notepad. "I know what you mean, Mrs. Smith. These nuances in behavior or speech can sometimes give more away than the words themselves. I'll have a talk with Mrs. Basket. Meanwhile, I'd like you both to be very careful. We don't yet know the motive for Don's murder or how dangerous this might get. Go home, put your feet up. You don't need to get involved with this one. It has nothing to do with your Amish community and I don't need your help. Okay?" He looked at them pointedly, until they both agreed.

As they walked out of the police station, Elsa-May's cheeks were still burning from embarrassment. She turned to Ettie, her eyes narrowing. "What were you thinking, telling me to sit in that chair? I looked like a fool!"

Ettie, unfazed, shrugged. "It was a comfy chair, wasn't it?"

"Well, it was comfy until Detective Kelly walked in on me drinking *his* coffee! I thought I was going to be arrested!"

Ettie rolled her eyes. "Oh, please. He wasn't going to arrest you. Besides, you did look pretty ridiculous with that coffee cup halfway to your mouth. It was kind of funny."

Elsa-May stopped in her tracks and glared at her sister. "Funny? You think this is a joke? We're in the middle of a murder investigation, Ettie!"

Ettie put her hands on her hips. "Well, maybe if you weren't so stiff all the time, you'd see the humor in things. We're trying to solve a mystery, yes, but that doesn't mean we can't have a little fun along the way."

"Fun?" Elsa-May repeated, incredulous. "People's lives are at stake."

Ettie sighed. "You need to relax a bit. Getting worked up won't help anyone, least of all us."

Elsa-May took a deep breath, trying to calm herself. "Alright, alright. Maybe I overreacted. But next time, can you please not encourage me to do something so...so silly?"

Ettie smirked. "Deal. But you have to admit, it was a little teeny tiny bit funny."

Despite herself, Elsa-May couldn't help but smile. "Maybe just a little. Anyway, let's go home. We'll need to find a taxi."

"Okay, but no more sitting in Kelly's chair or drinking his coffee."

Elsa-May nodded, smiling just a little. "Agreed."

THAT EVENING, Ettie and Elsa May poured over the information they had gathered so far, reflecting on the possible motives and suspects in Don's murder.

"Mrs. Basket certainly gave us something to think about," Ettie mused, her eyes fixed on the flickering flames of the fireplace. "And her mentioning his enemies was odd, but it might be helpful. I wonder if she'll tell Kelly what she told us."

"It's clear that there is more to this case than meets the eye. Was she giving us proper leads or was she just trying to throw any suspicion off herself?"

"The question is, why didn't you mention this Cedric Zabrik fellow to Detective Kelly?"

"The answer is, Ettie, I was waiting for you to say it."

Elsa-May picked up her knitting. "We will have to go there tomorrow."

"Where?" Ettie picked up her binoculars and stared at Elsa-May who was too engrossed in her knitting to notice.

"We'll go to Cedric's post office and maybe we'll talk with him."

"Good idea," Ettie said as she continued looking at everything around the room through her binoculars.

Elsa-May looked up. "Oh, Ettie, will you put those useless things away?"

Ettie lowered her latest possession. "They aren't useless, I just spotted a cobweb up there in the corner. I'll get it down tomorrow."

Elsa-May simply shook her head and kept knitting.

CHAPTER 12

The next morning, as the sun filtered through the crisp autumn air, Ettie had an idea. "Let's go bird watching."

"No, Ettie. We must talk with Zabrik."

"He'll still be there tomorrow. I think we both need a change of scene."

"All right. If it'll keep you happy I'll do it."

"Excellent." Ettie clipped Snowy's leash to his collar. "Come on. Let's get going to see these birds."

Elsa-May, trailing behind with a furrowed brow, was less enthusiastic. "Bird watching, eh?"

"Yes, and you'll enjoy it. Just you wait and see." Ettie put the bird watching glasses around her neck. "Thanks for coming with me."

"I'll never hear the end of it if I don't."

"Correct." Ettie gave a little laugh.

As they entered the woodland pathway, the canopy

of leaves overhead rustled softly. Ettie lifted the binoculars, scanning the treetops. Her eyes lit up as she spotted a flurry of activity—a group of American robins darting through the foliage, their red breasts a vivid contrast against the green leaves.

"Look at that, Elsa-May! And there—blue jays!" Ettie called out.

"They are pretty." A little further along they saw a pair of cardinals. "I suppose it's not all dreary," Elsa-May said, taking the binoculars from Ettie to have a look. Through the lens, she saw a woodpecker tapping rhythmically on a distant tree, its methodical process a stark reminder of the persistence needed in their own investigations. "I can't believe how much we can see." Elsa-May handed the binoculars back to Ettie.

"Bird watching helps me clear my head just like you said it would," Ettie confessed as they walked further into the woods, Snowy sniffing enthusiastically at the undergrowth. "It's peaceful here, away from all the complications of what we've been dealing with lately."

Elsa-May nodded. "I guess I needed this too. To just breathe and not think about back doors and stolen keys."

Their conversation meandered like the path beneath their feet, touching on lighter memories of past excursions and the simple pleasures of their shared childhood. It was a necessary reprieve, a momentary release from the tension that had tightened around the mystery of Don's untimely death.

As they made their way around a bend, a sudden rustle in the bushes caught Snowy's attention, and the dog darted forward, tugging at the leash with uncharacteristic urgency. Ettie, caught off guard, stumbled slightly but regained her balance as Elsa-May helped steady her.

"What's gotten into him?" Elsa-May wondered aloud, peering into the thicket where a frightened rabbit had now made a swift escape. Snowy, realizing his quarry was gone, settled back with a soft, disappointed whine.

Laughing, Ettie patted Snowy's head. "He wants to run free. I'm sorry but that's not possible, Snowy."

As they headed back, Ettie's mind wandered back to the unresolved threads waiting for them. "I don't know where to go from here. I can't help thinking that there is something we've missed or something we have overlooked."

"We'll figure it out. Today, we rest. Tomorrow, we'll go and visit Detective Kelly and see what he has found out."

"Okay, but which way is home?" Ettie looked around, turning in a full circle.

"We must have wandered deeper into the woods than we intended. I think we might be a bit lost."

"I think you're right. Let's keep walking and see if we can find a familiar landmark."

They trudged on, and after a few minutes, they came to a clearing. Ettie stopped and raised her binoculars, scanning the horizon. "Look over there," she said, pointing. "Do you see that fenced group of buildings in the distance?"

Elsa-May's mouth turned down at the corners. "There shouldn't be anything out here. This part of the woods is supposed to be empty."

Ettie adjusted her binoculars and looked again. "Wait a minute, I see people behind the fence. That's odd."

"What's odd?"

"They're wearing white suits."

Elsa-May squinted. "White suits? What on earth...? Do you think we've stumbled upon some secret government agency? I've read about them."

Before Ettie could respond, a loud buzzing filled the air. They both looked up just in time to see something large swooping down toward them. Snowy barked at it in a high-pitched tone, clearly agitated by the strange intruder.

"What type of bird was that?" Ettie asked covering her head as the object quickly rose.

Elsa-May's gaze followed the object as it turned and came back at them. "Ettie, it's a drone. It's a remote-controlled flying device. I've read about them."

"You seem to read a lot." The drone made another pass, dipping lower this time. Ettie's heart raced. "Why is it following us?"

Elsa-May grabbed Ettie's arm. "I don't know, but we need to get out of here. Run, Ettie, run!"

They sprinted back into the undergrowth, with Snowy out in front. The forest seemed closed around them as they ran, branches snagging their clothes and leaves whipping their faces.

"Is it still following us?" Ettie called out.

"I'm not sure, but keep running!"

After what felt like an eternity, they burst through the thick cluster of bushes and onto a familiar path. They both skidded to a halt, panting heavily. Even Snowy was panting.

Elsa-May looked up in the sky. "It's gone."

"We made it," Ettie gasped, bending over to catch her breath. "I can't believe that thing was chasing us."

Elsa-May leaned against a tree, her face flushed. "That was too close for comfort. I never want to see another drone again."

Ettie nodded, still breathing hard. "What do you think that place was? And why were they so interested in us?"

"I don't know," Elsa-May said, shaking her head. "But whatever it was, it's best if we don't go back there. It could've been a secret agency like I said. The drone might have been their security. Let's just go home."

As they walked back along the familiar path, the adrenaline from their encounter began to fade. "Do you think we should tell anyone about this?" Ettie asked, glancing at her sister.

Elsa-May considered that idea for a moment. "Maybe we should keep it to ourselves for now. We don't want to cause any unnecessary trouble. Let's just focus on getting home and putting this behind us."

As they finally reached the edge of the woods and saw their home in the distance, they both let out a sigh of relief.

"Well, that was quite the adventure," Ettie said with a small smile.

Elsa-May chuckled. "I'll agree with that. Next time, let's stick to the usual bird watching spots. At least Snowy and I have had our exercise for the week."

"I'll agree with that."

CHAPTER 13

*E*arly the next morning, a knock on the door jolted Ettie and Elsa-May from their breakfast. Ettie, with a curious glance at her sister, got up to answer it. Standing on their porch was Detective Kelly, looking as serious as ever.

"Good morning, Detective," Ettie greeted, stepping aside to let him in. "Please, come in and sit down."

"Morning, ladies," Kelly replied, stepping inside. He took a seat at their kitchen table, and Ettie poured him a cup of coffee. "Any progress on the case?" she asked, taking her own seat across from him.

Kelly reached into his coat pocket and pulled out a photograph. "Actually, I'm here about something else," he said, sliding the photo across the table. "Do you know these people?"

Ettie and Elsa-May leaned in to get a better look. Their eyes widened in surprise when they saw a picture of themselves, clearly taken from above, running through the woods.

"That's us. That was yesterday, when we got lost in the woods," Ettie said.

Kelly nodded. "This photo was taken by a drone. Can you tell me why you were in that particular vicinity?"

"We were bird watching," Ettie explained. "We wandered off the usual path and found ourselves in that clearing and the fenced group of buildings was in the distance."

Elsa-May looked thoughtful for a moment before asking, "Is it a secret government facility or something? We give you our word we won't tell anyone."

Ettie nodded eagerly. "Yes, you can trust us with secret information. I saw people in white suits, Detective."

Kelly threw his head back and laughed, a deep, hearty sound that filled the kitchen. "A secret government facility?" he said between chuckles. "Ladies, what you saw were naked people. It's a nudist colony."

Ettie's eyes widened in horror. "Naked people? But they were wearing white suits!"

"No," Kelly said, wiping a tear of laughter from his eye. "What you saw were people who weren't wearing anything at all."

Ettie frowned. "Those poor people have no clothes. Maybe you can knit them some, Elsa-May."

Kelly explained, still smiling, "They prefer to be

without clothes. It's a lifestyle choice. They're out in the middle of nowhere to avoid being disturbed."

Elsa-May shook her head. "Each to their own, but they must get cold in winter."

Kelly nodded. "They thought you two were a couple of peeping Toms."

Elsa-May covered her mouth in embarrassment, her cheeks turning bright red. "Oh my, we had no idea."

"It's alright. They were just concerned about their privacy. They weren't expecting a couple of Amish bird-watchers to stumble upon their retreat."

Elsa-May didn't know where to look. "Well, we'll be more careful next time. We certainly don't want to cause any more misunderstandings."

"I'm sure you won't. Just stick to the usual bird watching spots, alright?" He put his cup up to his lips and took a mouthful of coffee.

Ettie nodded vigorously. "Absolutely, Detective Kelly. We'll stay clear of that area from now on. Bird watching is new for me, but we will work out an area that we can use."

"One close to home," Elsa-May added. "So, any more progress in Don's murder investigation?"

"We're following leads. No break in the case so far." He continued drinking his coffee.

Once Kelly was ready to leave, they followed him to the door. "Thank you for clearing the whole nudist thing up for us, Detective Kelly," Ettie said.

He laughed. "Not a problem. When they called in

the complaint, I happened to be the first one to see it. I recognized you both and I explained to them it had to be an innocent misunderstanding."

"Yes, and can you tell them Ettie's sorry for the trouble she caused?"

"Me? We were both there, Elsa-May."

"You were the one who said the people were wearing white suits."

"Thanks for the coffee," Kelly said. "You ladies take care now."

After he left, the sisters sat back down at the table, shaking their heads in disbelief.

"Well, that was quite the adventure we had yesterday," Ettie said with a grin.

Elsa-May sighed, still a bit flustered. "I never thought we'd end up spying on a nudist colony. I'm just glad it's all sorted out."

Ettie nodded. "I'm glad you said 'we' were spying. Not just me like you said just now."

Elsa-May chuckled. "I just like to tease you in front of the detective. It makes you so flustered. It's amusing to watch."

"Is that so? Two can play at that game."

Elsa-May's eyebrows rose thinking about what Ettie might do.

CHAPTER 14

*E*ttie and Elsa-May arrived at the post office, Zabrik's place of work, hoping to talk with him. However, their hopes were dashed when they were informed by the clerk that Zabrik was on vacation.

"Vacation? That's odd," Elsa-May remarked to her sister once they were out on the pavement.

"The timing raises suspicion." Ettie agreed. "Especially considering the circumstances. It seems rather convenient, doesn't it?"

"We need to find Zabrik. We can't let him slip away," Elsa-May said.

"Agreed. We need answers, and we need them now. Let's see if we can get a phone book at the post office."

"Oh, good idea. I have seen a copy there for anyone to access."

They went back into the post office and flipped

through the phone book and were delighted to see his address. "I know where this is," Ettie whispered.

"Me too and it's not far away. Let's go. Let's hope he hasn't traveled anywhere."

Once outside, they slipped into the backseat of a taxi just after someone had gotten out. Ettie gave the driver the address and they set off. As the taxi bumped along the road, they discussed the peculiar circumstances surrounding Zabrik's sudden vacation.

"I mean, did he leave before or after the incident? And had it been planned? And has anyone checked if he's left the country? Oh, I forgot. No one would've done that because you didn't tell Detective Kelly about him."

Ettie sighed. "Well, how was I to know he was going to go on vacation? If I knew yesterday, I would've told Kelly."

Their conversation was interrupted by the taxi driver announcing their arrival at their destination, a small farm. As they stepped out of the vehicle, they were greeted by the green fields with grazing cows. A farmhouse stood tall against the backdrop of rolling hills, its weathered exterior hinting at years of history and a severe lack of maintenance.

Approaching the front door, Elsa-May raised her hand to knock, but Ettie hesitated. "Wait," she said, scanning the surroundings. "There must be someone here to look after the farm. Look at those cows grazing in the field."

Elsa-May followed Ettie's gaze and nodded in agreement. "You're right. We'll soon find out if you let me knock. Can I do that now?"

"Go ahead," Ettie said.

After a second and a third knock, they knew no one was home, or at least no one was coming to the door.

Ettie stepped down from the porch and lifted up her trusty bird watching binoculars. Peering through the lenses, she scanned the field and spotted a figure in the distance. "There he is," she whispered, her heart pounding with anticipation. "That's Zabrik."

"But you don't know him. How can you know that's him?"

"He's as bald as a bowling ball, remember?"

"Ah yes. That's right. Give me a look through those things."

Ettie moved them away from her sister. "No. They're useless, aren't they?"

Elsa-May grunted. "Let's go talk to this fellow." As they approached, Zabrik seemed engrossed in his work, unaware of their presence. "Excuse me, Mr. Zabrik?" Elsa-May called out, her voice carrying across the field.

Zabrik turned, surprise flickering across his face as he looked up. "Can I help you?"

"We have some questions for you about Don Friesen," Ettie blurted out.

Mr. Zabrik 's gaze hardened. "You do know you're on private property, don't you?"

Ettie realized how they must've come across to him.

"Oh, forgive us. We've been through a lot to find you and we didn't mean to sound rude."

"Who sent you?" he snapped.

"No one," Elsa-May said. "Forgive my sister. She always speaks first and thinks later."

He smiled at Elsa-May. "I know how that can be. I had a sister myself once."

Ettie stared at him. What happened to his sister? Did he kill her too?

"I've heard about what happened to Don. Everyone in town is talking about it. A tragedy indeed. But what does it have to do with me?" he asked.

Elsa-May took a step closer, her eyes meeting Mr. Zabrik's. "We understand there was a long-standing dispute between you and Don regarding a land boundary. Can you shed some light on your relationship with him? The reason we are here is because someone mentioned your argument with Don and—"

"That man was nothing but trouble. Always trying to encroach on my land, claiming it was rightfully his. We had countless arguments, and it escalated to the point where legal action was taken. But murder? No, I had no part in that."

Ettie and Elsa-May exchanged a glance, sensing a genuine frustration in Mr. Zabrik's words.

"I see," Ettie said as she rubbed her chin trying to come up with another question.

"Who mentioned my name? It was Basket, wasn't it? She's a basket case for sure. Meaning she's not all there. We used to call people like her basket cases in my day."

"I believe her name is pronounced Bask-kay." Elsa-May noticed a fence next to her and leaned against it.

"Nah, she's just trying to sound posh to help her flog off that junk she's selling. If you're trying to find out who killed him, you should ask the basket case."

"We already have," Ettie said. "But before someone else points the figure in your direction—" Ettie started, but Elsa-May interrupted with a nudge.

"You mean finger, Ettie. 'Points the finger' in your direction," Elsa-May whispered.

Ettie frowned, considering the words. "No, I'm sure it's figure. Because when you point the figure, you're figuring things out."

Elsa-May couldn't help but laugh. "That's not even close, Ettie. It's points the figure. Oh, now you have me saying it. It's points the finger!"

"I believe it *is* points the finger," Zabrik interjected, putting an end to the debate and silencing the two sisters.

Ettie put her hand to her head. "Now, I've lost my train of thought entirely."

"What my sister would say, if her brain would allow her, is that these disputes with Mr. Friesen, they must have caused quite a stir in your life, a disruption that was hard to overlook."

He shifted from one foot to the other, the lines on his face deepening. "Disruptions, yes, but not enough to end a man's life. We're all God's children; we settle our disputes according to His laws. That's what the laws of the land are based on are they not?"

"But human emotions often blur the lines of righteousness, don't they?" Ettie chimed in. "Anger, pride, greed—"

"Are you suggesting I let these sins guide me?" Mr. Zabrik 's voice rose, a tinge of anger seeping through. The cattle behind him shuffled, picking up on the unrest.

"Not at all. We're merely trying to understand the full picture. People are complex, and in times of stress, they might act out of character."

Zabrik sighed, his shoulders slumping slightly. "You don't know what it was like. Friesen was a thorn in my side, yes. But he was once a friend. His stepson played with my son; our lives intertwined in ways you couldn't possibly understand." As he spoke, his expression softened, revealing a glimpse of the vulnerability hidden beneath his rugged exterior.

"What happened to the two of you? Where did it all go wrong?" Elsa-May asked.

"Simple. He wanted my land," Mr. Zabrik continued, his gaze distant, perhaps viewing a past event in his mind's eye. "Said it belonged to his family first. We were at loggerheads for years. Court meetings, legal letters... it drained me."

"So, it wasn't just a boundary dispute?"

"No. It was more than that," he insisted.

Elsa-May placed a comforting hand on his arm. "It sounds stressful."

"It was..." He paused, lost in his recollections. "But I didn't kill him. I didn't."

"Mr. Zabrik," Ettie ventured, "did Mr. Friesen have any dealings that you were aware of, outside of the land dispute? Any other people he rubbed the wrong way?"

His eyes narrowing as he delved into his memories. "Friesen had his fingers in many pies. He was always looking for the next big opportunity. That alone made him some enemies, I reckon."

"Enemies within the antiques circle, perhaps?" Elsa-May prodded gently, thinking of the mysterious key.

"Possibly," he conceded. "There were whispers. He'd found something, something valuable. Got the whole town talking. That kind of chatter doesn't always attract the right kind of people. I heard he was telling people about a big break, something that would settle all his debts and then some."

Ettie leaned in, intrigued. "Did he mention what it was?"

"Just that it had to do with some old thing he'd gotten his hands on. Said it was going to allow him to retire." Mr. Zabrik shook his head as though he didn't believe a word. "I thought it was all talk, you know? He was always an attention seeker, so I paid no mind and maybe no one else did either."

Elsa-May, feeling a pulse of intuition, asked, "Did

you ever see him with anyone unusual? Strangers in town, perhaps?"

"No, but if you're looking for strangers there will be plenty of them at the antique fair."

Ettie's eyes opened wide. "Antique fair? When is that on?"

"It's on at the community centre. It starts on Friday and goes all weekend. Don would've been there, and the 'basket case' will definitely be there. Antique dealers come from all over. You might find out something if you ask his cronies."

Elsa-May nodded. "Thank you. We'll go to that fair, won't we, Ettie?"

"Yes. It seems likely."

"I wish you well, ladies."

"Thank you." Ettie saw a cell phone sticking out of his pocket. "Would you mind calling us a taxi?"

"Certainly." He called them a taxi and as he was putting the phone back in his pocket he said, "I did hear a rumor if you're interested."

Elsa-May and Ettie stared at him waiting for him to continue.

"Don's ex-wife will be running a stall at the fair in his place. I've heard she's taking over his store. How's that for a weird tide-turning situation?"

"It certainly is interesting," Ettie said.

He grinned at them. "Maybe you should 'point the figure' at her."

Ettie gave an embarrassed laugh.

"Goodbye ladies."

"Thank you for the insights, Mr. Zabrik. We appreciate your help," Elsa-May said before she looped her arm through Ettie's and they both headed back to the road.

CHAPTER 15

$\mathcal{B}$ack at Ettie and Elsa-May's home, they reviewed their findings at their kitchen table.

"Both Mrs. Basket and Mr. Zabrik seem to have strong reasons to hold a grudge against Don," Ettie said, her fingers lightly tapping on the table. "Their denials could be genuine, but they could also be lying."

Elsa-May nodded, her eyes focused on the suspects. "Indeed, Ettie. It's crucial for us to explore all possibilities and gather more evidence. There may be others involved, or perhaps there are hidden motives we have yet to discover."

"I'd say the antique fair might be useful. And now we have another suspect."

"We do. The ex-wife. Let's talk with her at the fair. And we still must go back and see the baker. She must feel dreadful now that the key was stolen." Elsa-May grimaced.

"We can do that tomorrow. Maybe we should have the baker sketch the key and we can ask the dealers if they know anything about such a key."

"Good idea."

Ettie added, "And don't forget the poem. I wonder if that's connected. And you still have those symbols written down, don't you?"

"I do, I mean, I did, but I think I lost them."

"Really?" Ettie shook her head in disbelief.

"No. I remember now. Detective Kelly took it. You were there at the time. Why didn't you recall that?"

"I did. I was just testing your memory."

"Oh, Ettie."

Ettie chuckled.

THE NEXT DAY, Ettie and Elsa-May returned to Mrs. Henderson's bakery, eager to delve deeper into their investigation. The bell above the door jingled as they entered, and Mrs. Henderson looked up from behind the counter with a bright smile.

"Good morning, ladies." Mrs. Henderson wiped her hands on her apron.

"We just want one minute of your time if we could," Ettie said.

Mrs. Henderson chuckled warmly. "Well, today's

your lucky day then. I happen to have just frosted a fresh batch of chocolate cakes. It's the 'cake of the day.'"

"Chocolate cake? That sounds perfect," Ettie said with a grin.

Mrs. Henderson ordered them to sit at a table and then she bustled about, slicing generous portions of the decadent chocolate cake and placing them on delicate floral china plates. She then expertly prepared two cappuccinos, frothing the milk to perfection and dusting the creamy foam with cocoa powder.

"Here you go, dears," she said, setting down the coffee and cake with a flourish. "On the house."

Ettie and Elsa-May exchanged surprised looks, touched by Mrs. Henderson's kindness. "Thank you so much, Mrs. Henderson," Elsa-May said gratefully. "That's really generous of you."

Mrs. Henderson smiled warmly as she sat down with them. "I suppose you heard that special key was stolen?"

"We did," Ettie answered because Elsa-May's mouth was full of cake.

"It was a shock." Mrs. Henderson looked out the window into the distance. "Then I got a second shock."

"What was that?" Ettie asked.

"I heard that Michelle and her son are now running Don's store. They've taken it over. Michelle is his ex-wife."

Elsa-May finished her mouthful of cake and then

said, "We only just heard that now, today. No wait, it was yesterday."

"And her son, he's been to prison you know," Mrs. Henderson told them.

"We didn't know that," Ettie said.

Elsa-May's eyebrows rose. "What did he do?"

"I'm not sure. But it just goes to show something. The average person doesn't end up in prison. I mean, I haven't been to prison. Have either of you been to prison?"

Ettie set her cup down. "Oh yes, I've been to prison."

Mrs. Henderson's mouth fell open in shock. "You've been to prison?"

Elsa-May frowned at her sister. "No, you haven't!"

Ettie shrugged. "I have. I've been to prison many times."

Mrs. Henderson's eyes widened in astonishment. "But... why? What for?"

Ettie leaned back. "I've visited people in prison."

Elsa-May couldn't help but chuckle. "Mrs. Henderson means have you committed a crime and gone to prison. She's not talking about visiting people."

Ettie gave a dramatic sigh, as if disappointed by the misunderstanding. "Well, if you want to split hairs about it..."

Mrs. Henderson smiled. "Oh, Ettie, you had me worried. I was about to call Detective Kelly to find out what you'd done. Now, what were we talking about? Oh yes, Don's ex-wife taking over the store."

"Well, we heard that she might not be an ex-wife because they never divorced." Elsa-May wiped the crumbs off her lips with a paper napkin.

Mrs. Henderson's expression darkened. "I can't tell you either way. But I can tell you she's not fit to run a lemonade stand, let alone Don's store. If she plans to stay, I'll be moving my bakery across town."

Elsa-May slurped her coffee. "Is she that difficult to get along with?"

"I never had much to do with her. She never came in here. I'm just going by what Don said about her. She was a difficult woman, but they must've made amends somewhere along the way."

"Sounds like you were very close with Don," Ettie said.

"It was wonderful to have him just next door. He'd always pop in to sample my latest creations, offering his honest feedback with a smile. He had a knack for flavors and a genuine passion for food."

"Do you have any idea who stole that key?" Ettie asked.

"If I had to guess, I would think that it could be Michelle's son. I mean, he does have a criminal record."

Ettie shook her head. "But that doesn't make sense. He'd need a reason, and how would he have known about the key? Or how would anyone have known about it?"

"I suppose Don could've mentioned the key to someone seeing he told you both about it. The puzzle of the key is frustrating. I fear we may never know about it or find out what it unlocked."

"Perhaps the killer thought Don had the key, and then well, maybe Don told him it was at the bakery," Elsa-May suggested.

"You could be right, and he knew the key wasn't going anywhere so he came at night and took it. And trashed the place while he was at it." Mrs. Henderson let out a loud sigh.

"Or she," Ettie added. "We can't assume the killer is a man."

Mrs. Henderson's eyes opened wide. "I was assuming it was Michelle's boy."

Elsa-May's mind raced with possibilities. "Don't worry, Mrs. Henderson. We'll try to find out what happened with that key, and who killed Don."

"No, don't you worry about it. Detective Kelly seems quite positive he'll get to the bottom of things. Now, how about another piece of chocolate cake?"

Ettie shook her head. "I couldn't possibly—"

"Yes, please," Elsa-May said lifting her empty plate.

Before they left, Mrs. Henderson insisted on them taking a bag of baked goodies with them.

CHAPTER 16

*T*he following day, after a breakfast of croissants and bagels from Mrs. Henderson's bakery, Ettie and Elsa-May prepared to leave their cozy home nestled on the edge of town. Pulling their scarves a little tighter, they turned to their two loyal companions.

Snowy danced around Elsa-May's feet, his tail a blur of motion. "Oh, Snowy, keep your paws warm today, won't you?" Elsa-May cooed, bending down to ruffle his fur. She offered him a small treat and he snapped it out of her hand.

Ettie smiled at Kelly, the cat. "We'll be back before you know it, and I'll bring you a both a treat. How does that sound?" She looked at Kelly and the dog, but Snowy was too busy looking for more treats to realize Ettie was talking to him.

Elsa-May straightened up and opened the front

door, her breath forming a misty cloud as she spoke. "Let's hurry up."

"Always in a hurry," Ettie muttered as she hung her trusty bird watching binoculars around her neck.

Elsa-May looked over at her. "Do you really need those today?"

"I do. They've already been valuable, and they will be again." Ettie sailed through the open door and Elsa-May closed the door behind them.

The sisters then proceeded to walk down their road to the shanty where they'd call a taxi.

After making that call, Ettie said, "The antique fair might just give us the answers we're after. It's strange to think how things are unfolding. One person leads to another, one story to the next."

"Yes," Elsa-May replied, her eyes thoughtful. "It's all happening so quickly. Mrs. Friesen taking over the store, the rumors of a valuable find. It doesn't sit right with me."

"Wouldn't it be funny if we found that stolen key today at one of the stalls?"

"Would you remember it if you saw it again, Ettie?"

"I certainly would. You know what we forgot?" Ettie asked.

"Yes. I was just thinking that we forgot to ask Mrs. Henderson to draw the key for us."

The sound of the taxi's arrival startled them. The sisters greeted the driver as they settled into the backseat.

The drive to the community center was quiet, each sister lost in her own thoughts about the day ahead.

Upon arrival, the place was already bustling as they approached, with vendors setting up and early birds browsing the stalls.

Elsa-May and Ettie made their way through, their eyes sharp for any sign of Mrs. Friesen's stall. It wasn't long before they found it, positioned prominently by the entrance, the wares displayed with evident pride.

"Excuse me, Mrs. Friesen?" Elsa-May said.

Mrs. Friesen, busily arranging a set of ornate silver spoons, paused and looked up. "Yes. I'm Mrs. Friesen."

"We're friends of Don's, and we heard about what happened. We're so sorry for your loss."

Mrs. Freisen's expression was guarded, but she managed a polite nod. "Thank you. Yes, Don's passing was unexpected. Me taking over the business was what he wanted so that's why I'm here if you're wondering." She looked around. "Like everyone else in this building is wondering."

"Oh no. We're not wondering anything like that," Elsa-May said.

"There hasn't been a funeral time arranged yet?" Ettie asked, trying to sound as gentle as possible.

"We would like to attend," Elsa-May added.

Mrs. Friesen's fingers hesitated over the silverware. "No, not yet. Things have been... complicated. The will, the business—it's all been moving fast. Were you customers of Don's?"

Ettie smiled and held up the binoculars. "I bought these from him."

Elsa-May leaned forward. "And let me tell you, she never goes anywhere without them."

Mrs. Friesen chuckled. "Let's not be so formal then. Please call me Michelle."

Ettie introduced herself and her sister.

"We understand these are challenging times," Elsa-May said softly.

Mrs. Friesen gave a tight smile, her eyes flicking back to her wares. "I appreciate your concerns. Now, if you'll excuse me, I have to attend to unpacking the rest of these goods."

As they moved away, Ettie whispered, "Nice work. You upset her."

"Well, you weren't saying much. We need to be watchful, Ettie. There's more here than meets the eye. Let's keep our eyes and ears open."

The large hall hummed with the quiet excitement typical of an antique fair, where every item promised a story and, if the sisters were lucky, every overheard whisper could turn into a clue.

After moving around and looking at all the stalls, they returned to Mrs. Friesen's stall only to find Michelle gone and a young man in her place. His posture was stiff, and he was wearing a crisp white shirt and a red tie. He had an air about him that seemed at odds to the casual bustle of the fair.

The sisters paused at the next-door stall pretending

to examine a collection of colored drinking glasses, but kept their eyes and ears tuned to the interaction at Mrs. Friesen's booth. They overheard snippets of conversation from other fairgoers, whispers that hinted at the young man's identity.

"That's her son, Craig," murmured one passerby to another. "Came back into town as soon as he heard about Don. Seems he's taking charge of things now."

Elsa-May leaned closer to Ettie, "He's Michelle's son."

When Mrs. Friesen returned, Ettie and Elsa-May's suspicions grew as they watched Craig interact with his mother. His tone was insistent, almost demanding, as he gestured toward a set of vintage watches they were displaying. Mrs. Friesen's responses seemed hesitant, her nods reluctant.

Suddenly, their conversation escalated. Though the sisters could not catch every word, the tension between them was evident. Craig's hand slammed down onto the table, causing a few of the watches to rattle against the glass counter. Mrs. Friesen recoiled slightly, her voice raised enough for Elsa-May and Ettie to catch a little more of the exchange.

"It's not just your decision, Craig. This was Don's life's work, not just some—"

"Mom, we need to think about the future. No one wants this old junk. Let's just sell what we can and get out."

Mrs. Friesen looked visibly upset, glancing around

as if to check whether they were attracting attention. She spotted Ettie and Elsa-May nearby and quickly composed herself, forcing a smile as she turned back to rearrange the watches.

Elsa-May tugged at Ettie's sleeve, nodding subtly toward a quieter corner of the fair. As they walked away, Elsa-May spoke softly. "He wants money. He doesn't care about Don's legacy."

"Well, if he's really not interested maybe he doesn't need to be involved. It sounds like Don might have left the store to them with equal shares. Otherwise, why would Craig be here at all?"

"He could just be trying to help his mother," Elsa-May said.

Ettie looked back at Craig. "And if Craig was really out of the picture until Don's murder, there might be more to his return than meets the eye. We need to find out if he had a good motive for wanting Don out of the way."

"Besides his inheritance?"

"Well, we need to find out how much that was and whether it was worth killing for."

"Where to now, Ettie?" Elsa-May asked, her voice barely above the low murmur of the crowd.

Ettie lifted her binoculars to her eyes—a peculiar sight indoors. She scanned the hall from their vantage point near the entrance.

"Ettie, what on earth are you doing with those?"

Elsa-May chuckled, amused yet not surprised by her sister's antics.

"One never knows what or who one might spot in such a crowd," Ettie replied, her eyes peering through the lenses. "Besides, these have been more useful than you will admit."

"You're going to find the answer to our mystery through those lenses, are you?"

"Maybe," Ettie quipped. "Or maybe I'll spot a rare 18th-century vase I can't live without." Their conversation was cut short when Ettie's posture stiffened. "Ah! Look over there, by the far wall," she whispered, lowering the binoculars and pointing discreetly.

Elsa-May squinted in the indicated direction. "What is it?"

CHAPTER 17

*E*ttie lowered the binoculars and whispered to her sister, "It's Mrs. Henderson, the baker, and she looks rather flustered."

Curious, the sisters approached Mrs. Henderson just as she was inspecting a display of vintage cake tins, her hands trembling slightly.

"Mrs. Henderson, good day to you," Ettie greeted her.

"Oh, Ettie, Elsa-May, it's good to see you both. I'm just trying to keep to myself today. It's all a bit much, really. How did you enjoy the little parcel I made up for you to take home?"

"Wonderful. Thank you. We had some for breakfast," Elsa-May said.

"Delicious." When Ettie saw her staring at Don's estranged wife, she added, "It must come as quite a shock to see Michelle and her son selling Don's antiques."

Mrs. Henderson sighed. "Indeed, it is. She's come back so boldly, as if nothing happened. And who gives her the right to do that? Just swoops in and takes over."

Ettie suggested gently, "Perhaps he left everything to her, Mrs. Henderson. After all, he had no children of his own, and they were married for quite some time, weren't they?"

"A few years, but it's the way she's done it. No grace, no respect for the grieving process. The ink on his death certificate isn't even dry, and here she is with her hands all over his stuff like he never existed."

The conversation paused as a group of attendees passed by, their laughter echoing off the high ceilings of the hall. Once they had moved on, Elsa-May leaned in. "Do you think there was something else, something valuable, that prompted her quick return?"

"Besides his death you mean? I doubt it, but Don was always talking about his discoveries. He'd think some things were special and then he found out the weren't. So, maybe she thinks she inherited more than she actually did."

Intrigued, Ettie exchanged a glance with Elsa-May. "And you think Mrs. Friesen might have thought there was something extra valuable among his collection?"

"It's possible."

Thanking Mrs. Henderson for her insight, the

sisters stepped away, their minds racing with new information.

"Ettie, do you think it's possible that Mrs. Friesen came back not for the business, but for something else… something more valuable?"

Ettie adjusted her binoculars, eyeing the bustling crowd with a new sense of purpose. "Anything's possible, but if he had something really valuable where is it?"

"That's a good point. Let's keep our eyes open and see what other secrets this fair might reveal."

While passing a quaint coffee stand adorned with vintage espresso machines and an array of pastries, they spotted Craig stepping up to order a coffee. Seizing the moment for a less formal interaction, Elsa-May nudged Ettie.

"Let's introduce ourselves properly," she suggested. They approached quietly, timing their arrival with Craig receiving his cup.

"Craig, isn't it?" Ettie extended her hand. "I'm Ettie Smith, and this is my sister, Elsa-May. We were friends of your father."

Craig, now with coffee in hand, turned with a guarded expression that softened slightly at the mention of his stepfather. He moved the coffee to his left hand and then shook Ettie's hand. "Yes, I remember seeing you at the store a few times. How can I help you ladies today?" He took a cautious sip, eyeing them over the rim of his cup.

He'd made up the bit about seeing them at the store, but Ettie figured he was trying to be polite.

"We were just so saddened to hear about Don," Elsa-May chimed in, her voice sincere. "And we've been hearing about your new responsibilities. It must be a challenging time for you."

"It is," Craig admitted, his posture relaxing as he leaned against the coffee stand. "Taking over hasn't been easy. There's a lot to manage, and everyone seems to have their own idea of how things should be done. I think we need to get rid of the store. Slash all the items by fifty percent. The place won't be the same without Don, so why force things? That's my opinion."

Elsa-May raised her eyebrows. "What does your mother think about that?"

"She's against it. She's always wanted the business, more so than my stepfather even, but when they split up, he didn't want her around the place."

Ettie nodded. "We can only imagine. We also understand that Don might have come across something quite special recently. It's the talk of the town." She watched Craig closely, looking for any flicker of recognition or discomfort.

Craig paused, his face unreadable for a moment. "I haven't heard that. My father was always finding 'special' things; it's part of what made him a good antique dealer. But if you're referring to rumors of some grand discovery, I can't really say. He liked to keep his cards close to his chest. I hope to keep his memory alive in some way, but it won't be through a dusty antique store. Excuse me, ladies."

After he moved away, Ettie and Elsa-May looked at each other. "Your thoughts, Ettie?"

"He doesn't want the store, but it appears Michelle does. If Craig is the killer, he didn't do it because he wanted a dusty antique store, so unless Don left him a heap of money, I think we can cross Craig off our list."

Elsa-May nodded. "And we know he doesn't want the store because we heard him talking with his mother. Let's go outside for a minute."

CHAPTER 18

*E*ttie and Elsa-May stepped outside, the cool air a welcome relief after the crowded warmth of the antique fair. They paused, taking in the tranquility that the outdoor setting offered compared to the buzz inside. It was in this moment of calm that they spotted Detective Kelly approaching the entrance, his brows raised in mild surprise upon seeing them.

"I knew you two wouldn't be able to keep out of this," Kelly remarked with a wry smile as he reached them.

Ettie chuckled softly. "Well, we thought we might spot a vase we'd like to buy."

Kelly nodded, his expression turning more serious. "Since you're here, there's something you might find interesting." He gestured for them to step aside, away from the few fairgoers who were beginning to leave, seeking a bit more privacy near a cluster of tall oak trees.

"Is this about Don?" Elsa-May asked.

Kelly leaned in slightly, lowering his voice. "Yes. I've been doing some digging into the relationships around Don. Turns out, Mrs. Basket and Don's ex-wife know each other quite well. They went to school together and have kept in touch over the years."

Elsa-May's mouth fell open, "Oh? How often do they keep in contact?"

"Very often. They both attended the same AA meetings here in town. Seems they've been supporting each other through their recoveries for a good while."

Ettie's mind raced with the implications. "So, they are close then? Could they have been in cahoots about something? Maybe about what happened to Don?"

Kelly shook his head, his expression turning slightly stern. "It's easy to jump to that conclusion, but we need to be careful about how we interpret their relationship. Just because they know each other doesn't mean they conspired together. It's important to deal in facts. We can't choose someone and try to make them fit the crime."

Elsa-May nodded, taking in his caution. "Sorry, you're right. It's just that every connection seems significant with how things have been unfolding."

"Understandable," Kelly conceded, his tone softening. "It's good to consider all angles, but we need to have facts not assumptions." The detective glanced back towards the hall, his gaze thoughtful. "I'll keep looking into their interactions, see if there's any evidence that suggests more than just a mutual support system. For now, though, it might be good to talk with some of the regulars at the meetings, see if anyone else noticed or heard anything out of the ordinary."

"That sounds like a prudent next step," Ettie agreed. "We appreciate you sharing this with us, Detective. It helps to have a clearer picture of the relationships involved."

"You're going to talk with them, or do you want us to?" Elsa-May asked. "We could go to the meetings and pretend Ettie needs help with her drinking issues. I'll be there as her support person."

Ettie's mouth fell open. "Me? Why don't you be the one who needs to be there, and I'll be the support person?"

Kelly chuckled. "Now, now. I didn't mean either of you to get involved with that. I'll question those people. Both of you go home and knit something, okay?"

Elsa-May grinned as though that sounded like a good idea, but Ettie wasn't so happy with his casual dismissal.

Kelly added, "If you hear anything, do let me know."

After they parted ways, Kelly headed into the community hall and the sisters hailed a passing taxi.

WHEN THEY GOT HOME, Ettie fell asleep on the couch. When she woke, she sat up and looked around. "I didn't expect to sleep. I was just going to lie down for a moment."

"Never mind. You must've needed it. I made you a cup of coffee, Ettie."

Ettie's face lit up with a tired smile. "Oh good. Denke." She looked around but there was no steaming mug in sight. "Where is it?"

Elsa-May nodded to the empty cup in front of her. "I got a little thirsty while I was waiting for you to wake up."

"You drank it?" Ettie asked.

"Yes," Elsa-May confirmed, shrugging slightly.

Ettie frowned. "Why would you do that?"

"I told you. I got thirsty."

Ettie grunted.

"Don't be grumpy. It's the thought that counts." Elsa-May grinned.

Ettie looked at the cup, then up at her sister, and a small, reluctant smile began to form. "You know, for someone who detests coffee, you sure have a knack for making it disappear."

Elsa-May laughed. "Maybe it's growing on me."

"Is that so? Well, next time, maybe leave a little for the person it was intended for."

"Okay," Elsa-May replied. "To make up for it I'll buy

our next meal when we go out. How's that for a peace offering? How does a slice of strudel sound?"

"All I can say is it's about time you paid," Ettie said, her voice now full of amusement. "But let's make it two slices. After the last few days, I think we deserve it."

CHAPTER 19

*T*he next morning, a sharp knock on the door announced Ava's arrival. Ettie hurried to open it, welcoming her inside.

"Morning, Ava," Elsa-May said, ushering her to the kitchen table. "We've got quite a bit to update you on."

As they settled down, Ettie began recounting their conversation with Detective Kelly. "So, he's got his officers questioning all of Don's customers, but so far, they haven't found anything useful."

Ava frowned. "I'm not sure why Don didn't tell you that I worked for him. And you mentioned he didn't even seem to know my name. Was he losing his mind or something?"

"Possibly," Elsa-May said, though she didn't sound convinced.

Ettie leaned toward Ava, curiosity burning in her eyes. "So, who do you think killed him? We know it

SAMANTHA PRICE

wasn't a robbery, so it would have to be someone who knew him."

Elsa-May sighed. "That's right, and Kelly has got his officers questioning all his customers, but as far as we know, they haven't come up with anything."

Ava nodded. "Joy does have a reputation of being unpredictable. Competitive, sure, but I've heard whispers about her dealings not always being... shall we say, above board."

Elsa-May sighed. "We need to tread carefully here. Accusing someone of murder based on hearsay and past grievances can have serious repercussions. We should talk to Joy, see if she's willing to share her side of the story before we jump to any conclusions."

Ettie agreed. "No one is going to accuse her, but I know what you mean. Let's visit her store later today."

As they formulated their plans, Kelly the cat leaped gracefully onto the table, her green eyes scanning the room as if she too were considering the mystery. Ettie stroked her head absentmindedly, then turned her attention back to Ava. "When you were working for Don, did you ever see Joy and him arguing or discussing anything at all? I'd like to know how they interacted. Any specific incidents that stood out?"

Ava thought for a moment. "Not that I saw personally. But there was tension there. I heard that Joy would undercut Don's prices or do anything to get his customers."

The room fell silent as they each considered the

130

implications. Snowy, picking up on the shift in mood, thumped his tail against the floor, breaking the momentary quiet.

Elsa-May stood, walking over to refill her tea. "We also shouldn't forget other possibilities. Just because Joy is an obvious suspect, we shouldn't narrow in on her. We need to find more clues and follow them."

Ettie nodded. "Yes, like Mrs. Friesen and even her son Craig. They've been acting peculiar since Don's death. Taking over the business so quickly, showing up at the fair... It's all very opportunistic. I mean, closing the store for a week or so, or even a day out of respect for Don, might have been the nice and proper thing to do."

"It would've been a nice gesture," Ava agreed. "But maybe they needed the money. Times are hard for everyone right now. I've been doing a lot of thinking about the killer. He could've been anybody come to rob the place or looking for cash, and then when he heard the doorbell chime when you two came in, he could've taken off."

Elsa-May shook her head. "People don't go around killing people for a bit of money. No. I can't help thinking that Don knew the person who murdered him."

Ettie sipped her coffee, her mind racing. "We need a timeline. When everyone last saw Don, and what he said to them. It's meticulous work, but it's the only way we'll uncover the truth. And we must do it while avoiding Detective Kelly. He'll only tell us to go home and knit."

Kelly jumped down from the table, her tail high in the air as if in agreement. Ettie watched her saunter out of the room, her steps silent and graceful.

Elsa-May giggled. "When you said Kelly, she probably thought you were talking about her."

"It is confusing that you've called the cat Kelly," Ava said with a laugh.

Ettie nodded. "I'm not sure why we did that. Anyway, let's go to visit Joy again."

"That's what you decided to do ten minutes ago, Ettie."

Ettie abandoned her coffee, picked up her binoculars and headed for the door. "Well, let's make it official then. The sooner we talk to Joy, the sooner we can get to the bottom of this."

Elsa-May and Ava followed, ready to uncover the next piece of the puzzle.

CHAPTER 20

*E*ttie, Elsa-May, and Ava stepped into Joy's antique store, eager to get their questions answered. Joy, however, seemed subdued today. She was standing behind the counter, her face pale and her eyes red-rimmed, looking visibly distraught.

Ettie's heart immediately went out to her. "Joy, what's the matter?" They had expected many things from Joy, perhaps defensiveness or even hostility, but not tears.

Joy hesitated for a moment before finally speaking. "I received a funeral notice for Don this morning. Someone shoved it under the door." She gestured weakly toward the crumpled piece of paper on the counter.

"Oh, Joy, I'm so sorry," Ettie said staring at the notice.

"It all seems so sudden," Joy murmured, her voice

echoing through the quiet store. "I knew he was gone, but I didn't realize how much it would affect me until now." She paused, taking a deep breath to compose herself. "The funeral is the day after tomorrow. The finality of it all has jolted me more than his death did."

They knew she was in no state to answer questions. Elsa-May took the lead. "Come, sit down," she urged gently, guiding Joy to a faded brocade covered armchair near the counter. "I'll make you a strong cup of tea. Sugar helps, or so I hear."

"I would love that." Joy gestured toward a makeshift kitchenette hidden behind an ornate Chinese screen decorated with intricate mother-of-pearl inlays.

As Elsa-May set about preparing the tea, Ettie and Ava remained with Joy.

Joy wiped her eyes and began to speak more freely about Don. "He was a complicated man, but he didn't deserve this end."

Seeing an opportunity, Ettie asked, "Who do you think could do such a terrible thing to him?"

Joy's face hardened. "His stepson. That's my guess. He's nothing like his mother. I get along well with her, but him—never. I heard Don left them both a significant amount of money. I think he couldn't wait for Don to die when he found out he was included in the will."

Ava's eyes narrowed. "There was talk that you held animosity toward Don after what he did to you—teaching him the business then him opening up around the corner."

"What? Is that correct? This is the first time I'm hearing about this." Ettie stared at Joy.

Joy sighed, a long, weary exhalation. "It's true. He started with me as an employee. Of course, I was upset with him for years after he left. But death, you know, it's a great reminder of what truly matters. Now I regret being so angry. I mean, what was the point? Yes, he did something bad, but I wouldn't have minded if I knew he was going to open his own store. It was the secrecy and calculating nature of it that hurt me."

Ettie nodded, understanding. The threads of old grudges seemed trivial in the shadow of mortality.

As Elsa-May returned with a steaming cup of tea, heavy with sugar, she handed it to Joy, who accepted it with a smile.

"Thank you," Joy murmured, cradling the warmth in her hands. The women sat in silence for a moment, the quiet punctuated only by the occasional clink of china and the distant sound of window-shoppers looking in the window.

Elsa-May looked at Ettie, who gave her a nod. The simple look that passed between them let Ettie know that Elsa-May had heard the latest revelation about Joy and Don.

Once the tea had been sufficiently sipped, and a semblance of calm had returned to Joy's demeanor, Ettie ventured another question. "Joy, did Don ever mention fearing anyone? Or did he seem worried in the days leading up to his... his passing?"

Joy pondered for a moment, her brow furrowed. "He was a private man, kept his worries close. But I did notice he seemed more... agitated recently. Checking over his shoulder, jumping at shadows. I thought it was just the stress of the business."

"How did you notice this? Had you gotten closer to him?" Ava asked.

"Unfortunately, I'd see him every day when I got my breakfast from the café."

"The bakery?" Ettie asked.

"Yes. I suppose it is a bakery, but seeing they have coffee and all that, I call it a café. He was there every morning too. I tried to go at different times, but that wasn't always possible."

As they continued to discuss Don, his life, and the mysterious circumstances of his death, Elsa-May did her best to remember everything.

"Did you hear about a key that he found?" Elsa-May asked.

Joy shook her head. "Yes, you told me about the key the first time you came into my store. Don was always fascinated by keys."

At that point, Ettie realized the thing that Don was fascinated by might have led to his death.

The conversation eventually wound down, and Joy, looking a bit steadier, thanked them for the tea and the company. "You have a way of making things seem a bit lighter," she said with a weak smile. "Thank you for your company. Will you all be going to the funeral?"

Ettie reached over and picked up the crumpled funeral notice.

"Where's it being held?" Elsa-May asked.

"At the chapel two blocks away," Joy said.

Ava sighed. "I'm sorry. I won't be able to go, but I'm sure Ettie and Elsa-May will be there."

"We will," Elsa-May confirmed with a nod.

CHAPTER 21

*A*s Ettie and Elsa-May stepped into the small chapel, their eyes quickly adjusted to the somber, dimly lit interior where the final farewells to Don were to take place. The chapel was simple, devoid of the ornate decorations one might expect at a funeral; even more striking was the absence of any nod to Don's Mennonite roots. The service was organized by his ex-wife, Michelle, and stepson, Craig, who had inherited everything and had taken the reins of Don's affairs swiftly after his death.

Ettie whispered to Elsa-May, "It's odd, isn't it? Not a single family member of his own here, and nothing that speaks to his heritage."

Elsa-May nodded, her gaze sweeping over the gathering. "Yes, it's almost as if Michelle and Craig wanted to erase that part of him."

They found a spot towards the back, strategically

chosen to observe the attendees. The sisters were not just there to mourn; they were there to watch, to listen, and to piece together the mystery of Don's sudden passing. As the service commenced, soft organ music filled the air, but the sisters' attention was elsewhere.

Joy Basket, the antique dealer, was seated in the middle row, her face a mask of solemnity. Not far from Joy, Mrs. Henderson sat dabbing her eyes with a tissue.

"Notice how Joy keeps looking over at Craig and Michelle?" Elsa-May murmured under her breath.

Ettie nodded. "And Craig doesn't seem to be grieving. He's too... composed, almost like he's attending a business meeting rather than his father's funeral."

"Stepfather," Elsa-May corrected her.

The service was brief, the eulogy delivered by a local pastor who seemed to know little about Don, his words generic and hollow. Ettie felt a twinge of sadness for the man they were there to remember, a man whose life's complexities were reduced to mere formalities in death.

After the service, as people started to mingle outside in a covered area where refreshments were being served, Ettie and Elsa-May approached Joy. She seemed surprisingly happy today.

"Joy, it was quite a service, wasn't it?" Ettie asked, trying to sound casual.

Joy smiled at Ettie and then glanced at Craig, who was talking animatedly with Michelle a few feet away. The smile quickly left her face. "Yes, but it wasn't what

Don would've wanted," she said quietly. "He valued his heritage, his simpler way of life. What happened today was Michelle and Craig's doing."

"But he left his family," Elsa-May said.

"No one ever truly forgets where they came from. It makes them who they are. There's no choice about that," Joy said.

"And how do you feel about the way they've handled everything since Don's passing?" Elsa-May asked, watching Joy's reaction closely.

Joy's lips thinned, "It's all been too quick, too cold. It's like they couldn't wait to put him in the ground and move on." Her eyes darkened, "Don deserved better."

Elsa-May cleared her throat. "We were told that you and Michelle get along, but the way you're talking it doesn't sound like it."

Joy's eyebrows rose. "Who told you that?"

Elsa-May shrugged her shoulders. "I can't remember now."

"If I'm civil to people that means I'm being cordial. In my line of business, I can't afford to make enemies. Seeing I have an antique store that makes me a public figure."

The sisters exchanged a look. Elsa-May noted this reaction, adding it mentally to the mosaic of information they were assembling. They thanked Joy and moved on to speak with Mrs. Henderson, the baker.

Elsa-May glanced back, catching a final glimpse of

Joy's expression, that was now troubled, before turning her attention to the next conversation.

The sisters approached Mrs. Henderson, who was still wiping away tears with a handkerchief. Her voice trembled as she greeted them. "Thank you for coming. It means a lot to see familiar faces today."

Elsa-May offered a gentle smile. "We wouldn't have missed it. It seems he was a friend to everyone in town."

Mrs. Henderson nodded. "He certainly was. Always the first to offer help."

Ettie wondered if Mr. Zabrik would agree and she looked around for him and couldn't see him anywhere.

The conversation paused as a group of mourners passed by, offering their condolences. Once they moved on, Mrs. Henderson continued, "It's just so sudden... all this."

"Yes, it is. Joy mentioned that today's arrangements weren't quite what Don would have wanted," Elsa-May said.

Mrs. Henderson sighed, a look of resignation crossing her face. "Don was a simple man. He loved this town, and its people. I don't think Michelle and Craig see things that way. They won't care about their customers the way that he did. They didn't understand Don at all."

"That's a shame," Ettie said.

Changing the subject, Mrs. Henderson asked, "I

hate to bring this up, but do you still think his death is something to do with the key?"

"We don't know," Elsa-May responded.

"It's odd to think that I will open my bakery tomorrow and life will continue just the same, but without Don there. I just wished I had never found the key or never told Don about it, at least. Maybe we'll never know the mystery surrounding the key or his death."

"Don't you worry, Mrs. Henderson. I'm sure Detective Kelly will get to the bottom of things."

Mrs. Henderson gave a relieved smile. "Just call me Elaine. Mrs. Henderson sounds so formal. Does Detective Kelly know anything yet?"

"I'm sure he does, but he often keeps things to himself until he makes an arrest," Ettie said trying to reassure her.

"It's true." Elsa-May nodded.

"I hope the person who did this to Don gets caught, and I hope justice is served," Mrs. Henderson said with a nod. Then something caught Mrs. Henderson's attention.

Ettie and Elsa-May looked over to where she was staring and saw Zabrik.

"I wonder if the detective has talked with him?" Mrs. Henderson whispered to them.

"Did Mr. Zabrik ever have any interest in keys or antiques?" Ettie asked.

"I don't know, but I know he had an interest in

money and in the last few years Don and he never saw eye to eye on anything. You might say that it doesn't mean that he killed him, but someone did. It could've been someone here at his funeral."

The three ladies looked at the sea of faces as a chill went up Ettie's spine.

"Let's go speak with him." Elsa-May looked over at Zabrik, who stood isolated by a window.

"I'll stay here. You two go. I don't want to even look at him," Mrs. Henderson said.

Ettie and Elsa-May made their way through the crowd, each step bringing them closer to Zabrik, who seemed lost in thought.

CHAPTER 22

"*M*r. Zabrik," Elsa-May said.

A forced smile creased his face. "Ah, you two again. This is a sad day, isn't it?"

"It is," Ettie agreed, her eyes searching his. "We were just speaking with Mrs. Henderson about Don... and about all that's happened."

Zabrik's gaze hardened slightly. "Yes, Don was a good man despite our differences. It's a shame what happened. I suppose there is good and bad in all of us. I might have been too hard on him, expected too much."

Elsa-May nodded, observing his reaction. "Mrs. Henderson mentioned you had some differences with Don. Over business, perhaps?"

"I told you all this the other day. I'd rather not talk about any of it. What does it matter now?"

Elsa-May moved in front of Ettie. "Forgive my

sister. She does get carried away with things. How are your cows? I hope they're doing well."

Zabrik chuckled. "Ah, the cows are doing well, thank you for asking. They keep me grounded, remind me there's life beyond these disputes and sadness. About Don, he and I had different views on every single thing, even for what this town could be. But believe me, I respected him, even if we disagreed."

"That's good to hear. Animals have a way of keeping us focused on what's important," Elsa-May said, thinking about his cow comment. "We have a dog and a cat, and they keep us busy and entertained at the same time."

Ettie nodded. "This is true. There is always some kind of job we need to do for them. Cleaning up after them, feeding them, letting them outside to do their business. You wouldn't have to worry about that with cows because they're already outside."

Elsa-May frowned at Ettie and nudged her slightly in the ribs in an effort to stop her rambling.

Zabrik looked between the two sisters. "And what about you two? Why are you so involved with what happened to Don?"

"He came to us about a key he found. He wanted to find out about it. We were the ones who found him on that dreadful day."

"A key?"

"Yes. But it's gone now, it was stolen."

He folded his arms. "Tell me about this key. I've

heard rumors that he found some kind of key before he died."

"Well, it was baked into a loaf of bread."

Ettie nodded, and added, "At Mrs. Henderson's bakery. And there was a poem that came along with it. Well, we think the poem went along with it."

"What did the key look like?" He asked.

"It was gold and it had small inscriptions in it. We wrote down the inscriptions, and we went to his shop to see if he'd seen those inscriptions, but it was too late to talk with him."

He hung his head.

Elsa-May took over. "The key was stolen from Mrs. Henderson's bakery. She was the keeper of the key."

Ettie shook her head on hearing Elsa-May say that again.

Zabrik looked over at Mrs. Henderson. Their eyes met, and then Mrs. Henderson hurried away. "I wouldn't believe anything she says."

"Oh really? Why not?" Elsa-May asked.

"She's got shifty eyes."

"Can I ask you another question?" Ettie asked.

"Sure. Go ahead and ask me anything. I've got nothing to hide."

"What does it mean for you now that Don's dead, with the land dispute?"

"Zero. I sold that land many years ago. Did I resent Don for me having to sell? Absolutely. Did I kill him? No. That's all I can say."

As their conversation ended, Elsa-May felt satisfied that he was telling the truth. Zabrik was a complex figure, and while his demeanor suggested nothing but cordiality, he had nothing to gain from Don's death unless he felt like he was finally evening the score.

The sisters excused themselves, leaving Zabrik to his thoughts. As they moved back into the crowd, Elsa-May whispered to Ettie, "What do you think?"

"I think he's hiding something," Ettie murmured back. "But whether it's related to Don or just the stress of his own issues, I can't say."

"Guess we'll need to keep digging," Elsa-May concluded, her gaze drifting across the mourners. Each face had a story and a connection to Don. "Ettie, let's throw out some bait and see if anyone bites."

"Okay, you cast the first line."

Elsa-May shook her head. "It's always me, isn't it?"

"Yes, because you came up with the good idea." Ettie pushed Elsa-May toward one of the food tables.

"We only met him the day he died, you know," Elsa-May confessed to a small group gathered near the refreshments, her voice tinged with sorrow. "He called on us about something peculiar—a key Mrs. Henderson found baked into her bread. It seemed urgent."

Ettie nodded, her eyes scanning the faces around them for any flicker of recognition or unease. "We went to his store to discuss the key, but found him..." Her voice trailed off, the memory of the scene in the back room of the antique store still vivid and unsettling.

A woman in the group, a cousin of Don's by marriage, leaned in and introduced herself. Then she added, "A key, you say? Don was always fond of his collections, but he rarely mentioned anything specific. What was so special about this key?"

"That's just it; we don't really know. He didn't get the chance to tell us," Elsa-May replied. "Whatever it was, it must have been important for him to reach out to us, virtual strangers, with such urgency."

The conversation was briefly interrupted as Michelle, acting as the host, invited everyone to share a few words about Don. One after another, friends and family spoke of Don's kindness, his eccentric passion for antiques, and his somewhat reclusive nature.

As the formalities waned, Elsa-May pulled Ettie aside. "We need to talk with Mrs. Henderson again. She might not realize it, but whatever was in that bread could be the key to more than just a locked box."

Determined, they found Mrs. Henderson quietly observing a photo collage of Don's life. "Mrs. Henderson, did Don ever discuss his collections with you or his friends?"

Mrs. Henderson, still fragile from mourning, shook her head gently. "Don kept to himself mostly. But, that key was odd, wasn't it? This might sound silly, but sometimes I felt he worried about who might come looking for some of his things. He was there alone with some valuable items."

Ettie thought back to the cabinet of valuables. "It's

funny you say that, but whoever killed him didn't steal a thing."

"That might be because you disturbed them. You left me, went to his store and that's when you found Don."

Ettie thought about that for a moment. "I didn't see a back way out and no one passed us in the store."

Elsa-May nodded. "Correct. No one passed us and we would've remembered that."

"There is a way out of his backroom. There's a door."

Ettie raised her eyebrows. "I never noticed it. Does the detective know about that?"

"I suppose he does. Excuse me, I see someone I need to talk with before they leave." Mrs. Henderson hurried away.

"Ettie, that means that we could've scared someone, and they left before they robbed him."

"Kelly doesn't think it's a robbery. It just doesn't make sense."

As they left the funeral, the weight of unanswered questions hung heavily between them. "We need to dig deeper, Elsa-May. There's more to this story, and I suspect Michelle and Craig might be at the center of it."

"Yes," Elsa-May agreed. "Possibly the key is what the killer was after. I just wish we knew the reason for his murder. To silence him about something? But what did he know?"

"Maybe the killer asked Don where the key was before he killed him. Then when the killer realized that Mrs. Henderson had the key, he came back and stole it from her."

"Hmm, something doesn't sit right with me. Why kill him for the key and not her?"

"I think we should both have a day off tomorrow and clear our heads. Maybe you need to relax and do some bird watching."

Ettie grinned. "I just might."

CHAPTER 23

The next day, under a sky heavy with impending rain, Ettie and Elsa-May made their way to the local police station.

Detective Kelly greeted them at the entrance. "Mrs. Smith and Mrs. Lutz." He nodded. "I was just on my way out to speak with someone, but that can wait. Let's speak in my office."

Once they were seated, Elsa-May dove straight in. "Detective, have there been any developments? Any arrests made?"

"No arrests yet. This case isn't straightforward. However, we are actively following several leads."

Ettie leaned forward. "Leads? Are they people we know?"

"We're investigating several of Don's associates and some family members who might have had financial motives or personal grievances," Detective Kelly explained, seemingly choosing his words with care. "It's a complex situation."

"And was there a back door in Don's back room? We never noticed one, but then we figured that's how the killer must've left," Elsa-May said.

"Yes, it appears the back door was indeed used around the time of Don's death," confirmed the detective, tapping a folder on his desk. "We found some prints, though they're partial. We're hoping to find some probable matches, but it all takes time."

"What about the key Mrs. Henderson found? The one that was stolen?" Ettie asked, hoping this clue held significant weight.

Narrowing his eyes thoughtfully, Detective Kelly nodded. "That key is a significant piece of this puzzle. We have a full description of it and we're in the process of tracing its origin and significance if any."

Elsa-May processed this information rapidly. "Could someone have killed him over what that key unlocks?"

"It's a possibility, but unlikely. There are all sorts of ways to open things without the proper key. We're still connecting the dots."

Silence enveloped the room, punctuated only by the distant hum of activity beyond the office door. The detective's phone buzzed, and he answered it. When he hung up, he looked over at them. "Please, excuse me for a moment. This call is related to Don's case. I'll be back shortly."

After he left the room, Ettie looked over at Kelly's

chair. "Care to have another sit in his chair? He'll be gone for at least a few minutes."

Elsa-May frowned at her sister. "Don't start. No, I won't do that again."

Ettie chuckled. "It was funny."

"Funny for you, not funny for me."

Upon his return, Detective Kelly looked more resolved but remained non-committal. "I need to go. I'll let you know as soon as we get the case wrapped up."

As they stepped outside, the rain sprinkled down around them.

"You know what we need today before the rain gets any heavier, Ettie?"

Ettie looked up at the sky. "An umbrella?"

"No. We need to shelter in that little café up the road. The one we always go to."

"Now that's the best idea you've had all day, possibly all week." Ettie looped her arm through her sister's and together they walked up the road.

CHAPTER 24

*A*s they entered, the warm scent of freshly brewed coffee and the sweet aroma of pastries enveloped them, momentarily lifting the heavy air of their recent discussions. The café, with its cozy setup and soft background music, felt like a small haven. Elsa-May led the way to the glass cabinet that displayed an array of treats—croissants glistening with a buttery sheen, muffins bursting with berries, and slices of rich, velvety cake.

"I'll have the chocolate éclair and a latte," Elsa-May declared, pointing at the treats behind the glass. She then turned to Ettie with a playful smirk. "And my dear sister will pay today."

Ettie, accustomed to her sister's antics, smiled and nodded to the lady behind the counter, "And I'll take a cappuccino and one of those apple turnovers, please."

With their order placed, Elsa-May picked a table by the window, the light casting patterns through the glass. Ettie joined her shortly, sliding into the seat across from her with a sigh. The café's cheerful buzz provided a gentle backdrop as they leaned closer, lowering their voices to discuss the case.

"It's all tangled, isn't it? The key, Don's murder, and now potential leads that seem to lead nowhere fast," Elsa-May mused, her gaze fixed on the passers-by outside.

Ettie nodded, her mind racing with details. "Yes, and we might have interrupted the killer. That back door..."

Their conversation paused as the waitress approached with a tray. She set down their coffee and pastries with a friendly smile. "Here you go, ladies. I saw you the other day at Henderson's bakery, didn't I?"

Surprised, Elsa-May responded, "Yes, that was us. You have a good memory."

The waitress leaned in slightly, lowering her voice. "Well, you were talking to Mrs. Henderson about Don, right? There's some talk around town you might find interesting."

Curious, Ettie encouraged her, "Oh? What kind of talk?"

"Well," the waitress began, glancing around before continuing, "people say that Don had a visitor that day before he died. Someone not from around here. They seemed to get into an argument. And whatever that key was for, it seemed to be a big deal."

Elsa-May's eyes widened with interest. "So, you know about the key?"

"Oh yes. It doesn't take time for news to spread around here."

"Do you know who the stranger was?" Ettie asked.

The waitress shook her head. "No, but they were seen leaving the bakery quickly. Didn't even take the car, just walked off fast toward the town center."

"It was a man?" Ettie asked.

"Yes. That's what I heard."

"Interesting," Ettie murmured, taking a sip of her cappuccino, her mind already threading through this new piece of information.

"I should get back to work."

"Oh yes. Thank you for what you told us," Elsa-May said.

When the waitress had gone, Ettie said, "That could mean someone knew about the key besides Don and Mrs. Henderson. Someone possibly linked to..."

"The murder, but we did mention the key at his funeral so news could've spread from there." Elsa-May took a bite of her éclair.

They spent the next hour in the café, not just enjoying their refreshments but also revisiting every detail they knew.

When there was a lull in the conversation, Ettie

picked up her binoculars and looked through the window at the world outside.

"Not here, Ettie. Didn't you get enough of that yesterday? All you'll see is pesky pigeons."

"You're being rude to pigeons. They're Gott's creatures too."

"So are snakes and so are... all the horrible creepy crawleys but that doesn't mean I have to like them."

As Ettie peered through her binoculars, she reached across the table and grabbed Elsa-May's arm. "Well, would you look at that."

Elsa-May leaned in. "What is it, Ettie?"

"It's Joy and Mr. Zabrik. They're talking, and it looks intense." Ettie's eyebrows raised in surprise. "You remember how he called her a basket case? Well, you wouldn't think that seeing them now. They seem like old friends."

Elsa-May frowned, trying to catch a glimpse. "Really? That doesn't fit. What are they doing?"

"Wait, see that? Joy just handed him something small and metallic. It shined for a second in the sun before he stared at it and tucked it away in his pocket."

"A key, perhaps?" Elsa-May suggested.

"Could be. Or something else just as important. They're moving away from each other now, looking around cautiously. It's as if they don't want anyone to know they're meeting."

Elsa-May sat back, her mind racing. "This changes things. Maybe Joy knows more than we thought, or Mr.

Zabrik is more involved than he lets on. At the funeral, he said something awful about her, remember?"

"I do. It's clear he was lying about that. And if he is lying about that, what else is he lying about?" Ettie lowered the binoculars. "We've got a new lead."

"Perhaps two new leads." Elsa-May said.

CHAPTER 25

*I*n the quaint warmth of their kitchen, Ettie was energetically chopping vegetables for their supper—a humble but hearty vegetable medley with rice. Elsa-May sat next to her drinking a cup of hot tea.

Thinking about their visit to the coffee shop earlier, Ettie said, "I told you those bird spy glasses weren't just a silly impulse buy."

Elsa-May, setting the table, let out a sigh. "I never said they were an impulse buy and I never said they were silly. I just said they are annoying the way you use them and they are."

Their light banter was interrupted by a firm knock at the door. "I wonder who that could be. I'll get it." As Ettie opened the door, with Elsa-May close behind, she saw Detective Kelly standing there.

"Evening, ladies. I've got some news," he said, stepping inside.

Just then, Snowy darted at Kelly, barking excitedly. "Snowy, not now!" Elsa-May exclaimed, quickly ushering the dog into her room and closing the door.

As they settled in the living room, Detective Kelly took a seat, only to have their kitty, Kelly, leap onto his lap with a purr of approval. Kelly, caught off guard, let out a surprised chuckle, gently petting the cat. "Seems I've made a friend," he remarked.

"It seems so." Elsa-May laughed as she sat down. "So, what's the news, Detective?"

Kelly's expression turned serious again. "I thought I'd ask you. I've heard around town that you've been asking questions."

Ettie opened her mouth to speak, but Elsa-May got in before her. "Who told you that?"

"Mr. Zabrik. He owns the local post office."

"Oh, well, we can tell you things about him," Ettie said.

Kelly put up his hand. "Firstly, I'll give you some updates since you continue to do what you want when you want."

Elsa-May looked over at Ettie and shook her head. "Yes, she does. She's always been like that. Well, what news do you have, Detective Kelly?"

"It's about the security camera at Mrs. Henderson's. The battery was dead when the robbery occurred. She'd forgotten to charge it—understandably seeing she's been so upset about Don's death."

"That's really unfortunate," Ettie responded sympathetically, then decided to steer the conversation toward their observation from earlier. "Speaking of leads, we noticed something peculiar today. Joy Basket, a local antique dealer, and Mr. Zabrik were together, quite chummy. She even handed him something that looked small and metallic."

"Joy?" Elsa-May blurted out. "Ettie, you told me it was Mrs. Henderson."

"No. It was Joy, the antique lady."

Elsa-May shook her head. "No. You told me it was Mrs. Henderson. We even had a conversation about how Mr. Zabrik said something horrible about Mrs. Henderson at the funeral."

"That's not right." Ettie looked up at the ceiling and tapped her chin. "My mouth might have said Mrs. Henderson, but my eyes saw Joy Basket."

Detective Kelly scribbled some notes. "Okay, so we possibly saw Basket or Henderson passing Zabrik a small shining object. Are you even sure it was even Mr. Zabrik, Mrs. Smith?" Kelly asked.

"Of course I'm sure. I know what I saw."

Kelly turned to Elsa-May. "And what did you see?"

"Nothing at all. Ettie was looking through her spy glasses. I couldn't see them at all."

Ettie smiled and proudly lifted her binoculars for him to see.

Kelly nodded. "It is Interesting how Zabrik's name keeps cropping up. I've spoken with him a couple of times already."

"We'll keep our eyes peeled," Ettie promised. "Anything at all, we'll let you know immediately."

"Good," Kelly nodded, carefully setting Kelly the kitty off his lap as he stood to leave. "Keep in touch."

After he left, Elsa-May opened the door to her room, and Snowy burst out, tail wagging ferociously. The energetic dog made a beeline for the spots where Detective Kelly had sat, sniffing vigorously as if trying to decode the detective's scent.

"Looks like Snowy's on the case too," Ettie chuckled, watching the dog's antics before starting to tidy up the living room. Elsa-May joined her, and together they straightened cushions and gathered dishes.

As they went about their nightly routine, the sisters discussed their plans for the next day. "We should probably stop by the bakery again," Elsa-May suggested, wiping down the kitchen counter. "See if we can casually bring up Mr. Zabrik in conversation. Maybe someone else has seen him around Joy or noticed anything unusual."

"Good idea. And maybe we should also swing by the library. If Zabrik or this mysterious visitor has local ties, there might be public records or old newspapers that could give us more insight."

"No, that would take forever. We need more direction than that," Elsa-May said.

Their conversation continued into the night as they sat in the living room, with a cup of chamomile tea to wind down.

"I've been thinking," Elsa-May began, her gaze distant, "about when we first met Don. Remember how he pretended not to know Ava? But we later found out she had worked for him for years."

Ettie frowned, her mind turning over the memory. "*Jah,* that was odd. Was he just playing dumb, or was he genuinely confused? If he was hiding their connection, there must have been a reason."

"Could be a clue there," Elsa-May suggested. "Or maybe it was nothing—just Don's old age catching up to him and he genuinely forgot."

Ettie nodded. "Like you forgot that I saw Joy talking with Zabrik and thought it was Mrs. Henderson."

"I'm sorry, Ettie."

Ettie placed her tea cup down. "Tomorrow, maybe we should talk with Ava and see if she's had any further thoughts on why Don pretended he barely knew her. I mean, surely he would've known we'd talk to Ava about his key situation."

"As I said, Ettie, it could be a clue. Anyway, time for some sleep. Goodnight."

"Goodnight to you."

As they headed to bed, their minds were filled with plans for the morning.

CHAPTER 26

*T*he next morning dawned bright and crisp, the kind of day that held the promise of revelations. After a quick breakfast of toast and tea, Ettie and Elsa-May set out, their steps brisk with purpose.

Before going to see Ava, they decided to go to Mrs. Henderson's bakery.

The bell chimed cheerily above them, drawing the attention of Mrs. Henderson, who was lining up her morning's work behind the counter. "Morning, ladies!" She greeted them with a smile.

"Morning, Mrs. Henderson. How are you holding up?" Elsa-May asked.

"Oh, you know, one day at a time," Mrs. Henderson sighed. "What brings you in today?"

Ettie leaned against the counter. "We were wondering if you've noticed anything unusual about

Mr. Zabrik lately. Or maybe seen him talking to anyone he's never gotten along with before."

"Like Joy perhaps?" Elsa-May chimed in.

Mrs. Henderson paused, her expression tightening. "Now that you mention it, he was here more often than usual last week. Always kept to himself, but I did catch him chatting with Joy outside. I've never seen them say a single word to each other. I forgot about it until you mentioned it just now."

Ettie and Elsa-May exchanged glances, their suspicion growing. "Interesting," Elsa-May noted. "Thanks for letting us know."

With a new clue in their pocket, the sisters left the bakery. "Before we go to Ava's place let's go to the library," Ettie suggested.

"You decide, I'm just following along."

The old building was quiet, the musty smell of books a comforting constant as they walked through the aisles. Ettie went straight to the archives section, pulling out local newspapers, while Elsa-May started on the computer, searching for any property or business connections between Don, Ava, and Mr. Zabrik.

Hours slipped by as they combed through articles and records, piecing together the social and business network of the *Englishers* of their small town. Ettie came across a few mentions of Mrs. Henderson in association with local charity events, always in the shadow of Don's more prominent presence.

"Hey, Ettie. Come look at this."

Ettie walked over and read over Elsa-May's shoulder. "Antique Revival: Don Friesen's Store Hosts Restoration Workshops. Local antique store owner Don Friesen is hosting a series of workshops aimed at teaching community members how to restore and preserve vintage items. The workshops, which have drawn a sizable crowd, are being co-organized by Ava Glick, who has been working closely with Don over the past year."

"And they have a quote from Ava, using her maiden name. That would've been her name back then. *'It's a great opportunity to learn and connect with our heritage.'*"

"That's weird don't you think, Ettie?"

"It is. Don did know her well, for sure if she helped organize events like those. Maybe Don was trying to protect her, or maybe there was something more that we don't know about." Ettie patted Elsa-May's shoulder. "Good work."

As the library clock chimed signaling the hour, the sisters gathered their findings and prepared to leave. The pieces of the puzzle were slowly forming a clearer picture, but each answer they found seemed to lead to more questions.

"We need to tread carefully," Elsa-May whispered as they stepped outside. "Who knows what we might uncover next."

"I'm sure Ava wouldn't have been involved in anything."

"I am too, but let's go to Ava's place and find out, *jah?*"

Ettie nodded. "Let's go."

"Okay."

～

AFTER THEY GOT out of the taxi, Ava came out to greet them. "Hello, what brings you here today? Have you found out something?"

"We did. We found a newspaper article in the archives of the library that we need to talk with you about," Elsa-May explained as they followed Ava inside to the cozy living room.

Once seated, Ettie started, "It's about Don. We found that he was holding classes telling people how to restore items and you were helping him."

Elsa-May nodded. "There's even a quote from you in the article."

Ava's expression grew thoughtful. "I never talked to a reporter. Don always had me sign things. He told me it wasn't binding me to anything, just helping him out. But it made me uneasy, all those papers, and that's one of the main reasons I left working for him. I was just young back then, and not sure who to trust."

"Did Don ever explain what those documents were for?" Elsa-May inquired gently.

Then Ettie asked, "So you think Don gave the reporter that quote on your behalf?"

"He must've. And to answer your question Elsa-May, he said they were just formalities to keep the business running smoothly. Something didn't sit right with me, so I eventually decided to leave and start fresh somewhere. I went back to studying for a while."

"That must have been a difficult decision," Ettie sympathized, noting Ava's discomfort.

"It was, but it led me back here and now I have a peaceful life. I was there as a helper at those classes mentioned in that paper. A helper only because I didn't know what I was doing. Don was the expert. I'm not sure why he thought a quote from me would've helped. Anyway, how are you doing with the investigation?"

"Well, we've been following several leads. There's been some odd behavior from Mr. Zabrik and others around town. It seems Don's death might be tied to more than just a simple dispute."

Ava nodded, absorbing the news. "Don was always involved in too many things. I worried it would catch up to him someday. But I'm glad I left when I did. I never had much to do with his ex-wife. Like I already said, when I was there, he was newly separated so I can't give you much information about that."

CHAPTER 27

The ride home from Ava's house in the taxi was silent. When the taxi pulled up outside their house, they got out not even noticing a figure waiting near their front porch.

It was Mr. Zabrik, his expression stormy, his posture rigid with apparent anger. Elsa-May's breath caught in her throat, while Ettie stiffened as she grabbed her sister's arm in fright.

"What are you doing at our home?" Ettie asked.

"I need to know what you've been telling Detective Kelly about me," Zabrik demanded.

The sisters exchanged a quick glance, a silent agreement passing between them not to let him inside. "We're not sure what you mean. We've only shared what we've observed—that you were talking to Joy Basket," Elsa-May said.

175

"Joy Basket is unstable! You saw us talking once and spun it into some conspiracy. Just because we're both on the art exhibition committee doesn't mean we get along." Zabrik glared at Elsa-May and then Ettie.

"Art exhibition?" Ettie inquired.

"Yes. It's on tomorrow night and I'd appreciate it if neither of you attend."

Ettie took a step forward. "Mr. Zabrik, we only report what we see. And it's odd, don't you think? Calling her a 'basket case' and yet there you were, looking quite friendly with her."

"Quite friendly indeed!" Elsa-May added.

His jaw clenched, and for a moment, the sisters thought he might escalate the confrontation. But after a tense pause, he scoffed. "You don't know what you're messing with." Zabrik turned sharply, stalking off their property.

After watching him get into his car, the sisters quickly moved into their house. "Well, that was unsettling," Elsa-May murmured as they headed inside, locking the door behind them.

"Very unsettling. Now we must go to that exhibition."

"Really, Ettie? He warned us not to."

"Exactly why we must go. He's scared. People only get that defensive when they feel cornered."

"I'm scared too. Scared that he knows where we live."

"Don't worry. There's two of us. If he's the killer, he can't kill two people at the same time."

Elsa-May's mouth turned down at the corners. "No. He'll kill one and then the other. We need to be careful, Ettie."

"I'll heat us up some soup for supper."

"Yes please. That'll help."

Ettie didn't know if her sister was being sarcastic or not, but she put a saucepan of soup on the stove.

As they ate their soup, they strategized their next moves. Their conversation about Zabrik was interrupted by the sound of someone at their front door. "Don't tell me he's back."

When they answered, they saw it was a uniformed officer who informed them that. one of their neighbors reported seeing them having an altercation with someone.

"We're alright," Elsa-May assured him. "It was nothing more than a difference of opinion."

"What was the man's name?" The officer retrieved a note pad and pen from his pocket.

"Cedric Zabrik. Detective Kelly knows him," Ettie said.

"I'll let Detective Kelly know. When he heard this complaint called in, he arranged for patrol cars to go past your house at regular intervals for the next couple of days."

"Oh, that is nice of him."

Elsa-May nodded in agreement. "Thank you for stopping by." The sisters waved to the officer before they stepped back inside, locked the door, and then headed to the kitchen to finish their supper.

CHAPTER 28

The next evening, Ettie was gathering her essentials ready for the art exhibition: paper, pen, and, of course, her beloved bird-spotting glasses that doubled effectively for people-watching. As she slipped them into a bag, Elsa-May came up behind her.

"Ettie, please, not the bird-watching glasses tonight," Elsa-May pleaded in a whining tone.

"What if there's someone we need to watch from across the room? They're perfect for that."

Elsa-May shook her head. "It's an art show, not a wildlife expedition. We're supposed to be blending in a bit more tonight."

"We're never blended in anywhere we go."

Elsa-May thought for a moment. "That's true I suppose, but let's try to rely a bit more on our natural charm and a bit less on the bird-watching gear. We want to get people talking, not make them wary."

"Hmm, natural charm, eh? I guess I could do that. Alright," Ettie relented with a small, playful roll of her eyes. "For the sake of art, I'll leave them. But if we miss out on something, I'm holding you personally responsible."

Elsa-May chuckled.

With a final, somewhat regretful glance at her glasses, Ettie placed them back on the small table by the door. They grabbed their coats and headed out into the cool night air.

During their taxi journey to the art exhibition, the siblings' conversation was dominated by their theories about Zabrik's unusual request for them to 'not' attend. They weighed up different possibilities, with one suggesting that Zabrik might be unveiling a surprise sculpture to do with keys while the other contemplated whether it could be a matter of him trying to conceal his friendships. The speculation continued until they finally arrived at the venue.

Upon walking into the same community hall that had held the antique fair, they noticed a far different energy. The art show was buzzing. Artists of all ages and backgrounds milled around, their works displayed in vibrant arrays that transformed the hall into a kaleidoscope of color and creativity. Ettie felt a pang of longing for her spying glasses as they entered, but she pushed it aside, focusing on the people and their conversations.

They started with a leisurely stroll through the

exhibits, complimenting the artists, and engaging in light discussions about techniques and inspirations. Ettie found that without the glasses, she was indeed more present in the conversations, catching subtleties in tone and gesture that she might have otherwise missed while peering through lenses.

As they rounded a corner, they came upon Michelle's display of antique paintings. The area was a hotbed of whispered opinions and not-so-subtle critiques. Ettie and Elsa-May exchanged a look, knowing they had found their first real opportunity of the day.

"Let's hear what the fuss is about," Ettie suggested.

"I'm right behind you." They edged closer to a group of onlookers, who were upset about the paintings and them being in the show.

Elsa-May moved up to a lady. "Excuse me. Why doesn't anyone seem happy about these old paintings?"

"This exhibit is supposed to be a showcase for local artists, not for artists who died a hundred years ago," the woman whispered to the sisters.

Another woman overheard and turned around. "She just does what she wants. I know that Don wouldn't approve of this."

Then the two ladies started talking, which allowed Ettie and Elsa-may a chance to move on. Ettie whispered to Elsa-May, "Michelle seems a very controversial person."

"Well, the choice to put those old paintings in the exhibition is outraging some people."

Before they got too far, they overheard an older couple discussing the antique paintings. "It's a beautiful collection, no doubt," the man said, his voice carrying a note of admiration. "But I hear some of the artists aren't too happy about it."

The woman, leaning closer to a landscape featuring a serene valley, added, "It's a shame, really. Art is art, though."

Among the murmurs, they heard the familiar voice of Joy Basket. She was talking to a group of people. "It's just not in the spirit of the event, is it? We're here to showcase what the artists have created. Tonight is about the artists, it's not the antique fair. That was last week."

Seizing the opportunity, Ettie nudged Elsa-May, and they made their way over to Joy, who was visibly annoyed. "Joy, are you talking about the paintings Michelle brought in?"

Joy turned, her expression a mix of frustration and forced smile. "Yes, they're... something, alright. I just think this should have been about the living artists who are trying to make a mark, not about Michelle lining her pockets."

When the people had dispersed and they were left with just Joy, Elsa-May lowered her voice. "Speaking of making marks, you mentioned Mr. Zabrik the other day, suggesting he might know something about Don's troubles. He seems to think you're quite involved yourself. How well do you know him, really?"

Joy's eyes flickered with a hint of defensiveness. "Zabrik? He's just someone I've run into now and then at these town events. We hardly know each other. And whatever he's saying about me, it's just to get the heat off himself. Excuse me. I've seen enough and I have an early start in the morning."

After the sisters said goodbye, they turned back to the exhibition and saw Michelle walking toward them. "Ettie, Elsa-May, do you like the collection? It's been in my family for years, but I thought it was time they were seen by others before I put them in the store."

Ettie smiled, "They're lovely, Michelle. They certainly add a different flavor to the show. How did you decide to bring them out now?"

"Oh, with all that's happened..." Michelle's voice trailed off, her eyes clouding over with a mix of sadness and resolve. "I guess I just wanted to remind people that there's history here, beauty in what we hold on to from the past. Don always loved those paintings."

"Not everyone's happy about it," Ettie told her.

"I've stopped worrying about what people say about me many years ago."

As Michelle moved on to greet other guests, Elsa-May whispered to Ettie, "There's more to this than just an art show. Michelle's move, Joy's reaction, Zabrik's deflections—they're all pieces of a bigger puzzle around Don's death."

Elsa-May frowned. "Didn't Kelly tell us Joy and Michelle were friends? Joy didn't sound like she liked Michelle very much."

"I noticed. She seemed so upset."

Before they could ponder further, they ran into Zabrik near the entrance. His face was drawn, and he looked worried. "Ettie, Elsa-May, I'm sorry about earlier. I told you not to come because I've been so upset and rattled by Don's death. It was so unexpected, and on top of that, Detective Kelly keeps questioning me about things. It's made me nervous."

Elsa-May placed a comforting hand on his arm. "We understand. It's been hard on everyone."

Zabrik sighed, running a hand over his bald head. "You know, people do get charged for crimes they didn't commit. I've read about it. The idea of being wrongfully accused terrifies me. I didn't have anything to do with Don's death, but Kelly's questions make me feel like I'm his major suspect."

Ettie nodded sympathetically. "We know you're innocent, Mr. Zabrik. But the best way to help is to answer all of Kelly's questions honestly. The truth will come out. It always does."

He managed a small smile. "Thank you for understanding. It's just been a rough time."

As they parted ways, the sisters reflected on the evening's events. "There's so much tension in the air,"

Elsa-May remarked. "Joy, Michelle, Zabrik... they're all hiding something I'm sure of it."

Ettie nodded. "And it's up to us to find out what. Let's get home and go over everything we know. Maybe something will stand out that we missed before."

CHAPTER 29

*B*efore Ettie and Elsa-May decided what they'd do the next day, Detective Kelly arrived at their home.

"Good morning, ladies," Kelly began. "I have some news. We have arrested Don's killer."

"Who is it?" Elsa-May asked.

"Joy Basket, the antique dealer."

Ettie and Elsa-May exchanged a glance, both surprised. "Not Zabrik?" Elsa-May asked.

Kelly sighed, shaking his head.

"Come and sit down. I need to sit down before I fall," Elsa-May said.

Once they were seated, Kelly continued, "Zabrik denies ever speaking to Joy about anything significant. He claims their meeting was a coincidence, nothing more."

Ettie bristled at this. "I saw them through my bird-watching glasses, Detective. It was no casual chat. There's something he's hiding, I'm sure of it."

Elsa-May nodded in agreement. "Could it be possible that both Zabrik and Basket are involved? It doesn't add up that she acted alone, especially with what we observed."

Detective Kelly paused, considering their points. "Joy denies any involvement in the murder. She insists she's being framed, though we found compelling evidence against her."

"And what evidence might that be?" Ettie asked, leaning forward.

Kelly hesitated, then relented. "It actually came from something you mentioned earlier, Ettie. We have a witness who saw Joy leaving the back of Don's antique store right around the time he was killed."

The sisters' eyes widened. "Who is this witness?" Elsa-May inquired, her voice tense with curiosity.

"I'm afraid I can't disclose that information just yet. It's still part of an ongoing investigation," Kelly replied, his expression unreadable.

Frustration mingled with intrigue in the room. Ettie, never one to back down easily, pressed on. "Detective, if Zabrik is involved, wouldn't it make sense to consider the possibility of a conspiracy? Perhaps they were working together, or maybe Zabrik is using Joy as a scapegoat."

Kelly rubbed his chin thoughtfully. "It's a theory we haven't ruled out. But without concrete evidence linking Zabrik to the crime scene or the murder weapon, our hands are tied."

"What about the object that Ettie saw Joy passing to Zabrik? Could it have been something related to the murder—perhaps it was the stolen key?"

"We got warrants and searched Zabrik's home and his place of work. Nothing was found that could be linked back to Don or his murder. I've told you more than once that we must go by the facts. Eyewitness testimony is good enough for me."

Ettie shook her head. "Something about this doesn't sit right with me. We appreciate you coming to update us, Detective, but we're not convinced the whole story has come to light."

Kelly stood, preparing to leave. "That's why we need sharp citizens like you two. Keep watching and let me know immediately if you find anything important."

As the detective left, Ettie and Elsa-May sat back down, a mix of emotions running through them.

"We're missing something, Elsa-May," Ettie murmured, her gaze fixed on the fading light outside.

"I know," Elsa-May replied. "And we're going to figure it out, whatever it takes."

"Well, if Joy is not the killer, the real killer will have their guard down now. Let's go shopping, Elsa-May."

"Ettie, how could you think of shopping at a time like this?"

Ettie's eyes grew wide. "Antique shopping."

"Oh." Elsa-May gave a nod.

CHAPTER 30

*E*ttie and Elsa-May stepped through the door of Don's antique store, their arrival announced by the bell on the front door.

"It's lovely to see the two of you again," a female voice said from within the depths of the dark shop.

The sisters looked over to see Michelle approaching them with a hammer in her hand. Elsa-May stepped back and pulled Ettie in front of her.

Michelle laughed and explained, "Oh, don't be worried. I've just finished hanging the paintings from the exhibition. Well, nearly all of them. I sold three and two are under consideration."

"Congratulations," Elsa-May said stepping out from behind her sister.

"Thank you. What brings you here today?" Michelle asked.

"We just thought we'd see how you are holding up with all the changes."

"I'm okay. Thanks for asking. I'm a bit sad that Craig went overseas suddenly. I wished he would've stuck around, but that's the young for you only ever thinking about themselves."

"Seems like odd timing, with everything going on." Ettie watched Michelle's reaction closely.

Michelle sighed, setting the hammer down on a nearby table. "Yes, well, he needed a break from all this... chaos. The shop, the accusations—it's all been too much. Now that they've arrested Don's killer, I feel like I can breathe again."

Elsa-May nodded. "We also heard about Joy Basket. It's quite shocking to think she was involved in Don's murder."

Michelle's expression darkened. "Yes, it is. But then, Joy always was a bit unpredictable. And now with her in jail..."

Ettie interrupted. "We heard she was a good friend of yours."

"We were cordial and that's that. Friends is too strong a word."

"Do you think anyone else besides Joy was also involved in his murder?" Ettie asked.

"I don't know. I'd hate to think so. His death has brought a lot of suffering. Poor old Mrs. Henderson is taking it hard. She's been more hostile toward me than usual. That woman has never hidden her disdain for Joy

—or for me, for that matter. She was always around, hovering around Don, always bringing him tarts and cakes to taste. I think she hoped to end up with him someday."

Elsa-May leaned forward, her interest piqued. "That's quite sad for her. That's why she's taken it all so hard."

Michelle chuckled bitterly. "He found her... let's just say, he didn't return her affections. He was always friendly and polite, but she definitely hoped for more."

Ettie's mind raced. "We still haven't solved the mystery of the key. Why was it so important and did it have anything to do with why she killed Don?"

Elsa-May nodded. "I think you'd probably have to ask Joy about that."

"What does it matter? She'll be in prison for a very long time. I don't think the key had anything to do with his death. It was all just bad timing. I think Joy had a little crush on Don too."

The room grew silent as the weight of this revelation settled among them. "So, everyone was in love with Don?"

Michelle laughed. "I'm not saying that. It was just the baker and Joy Basket."

When the phone rang, Michelle excused herself to answer it.

"We'll go now," Ettie called out as Michelle picked up the receiver. Then Ettie grabbed Elsa-May's arm, pulled her close and whispered, "I just remembered.

When we were here on the day that Don was murdered, the phone rang."

Elsa-May's lips turned down at the corners. "No, it didn't, Ettie."

Ettie shook her head. "I mean, no it didn't, but remember the phone was off the hook when we were looking for him? I picked up the receiver and there was no one on the other end of the line. They didn't say anything but I heard someone breathing."

"Ah yes. I had forgotten that."

As the sisters walked outside, they discussed their next steps. "We should talk to Mrs. Henderson next while we are here," Ettie suggested. "There's more to her story, I'm sure."

"Yes, and we need to tread carefully if it's true that she was in love with him." Elsa-May gave a sigh.

CHAPTER 31

As they walked the few steps to the bakery, Ettie thought about the key and the bread. "I don't believe that key was ever baked into any bread. It was placed there intentionally, Elsa-May, and I think Mrs. Henderson knows more than she's let on."

Elsa-May looked over at her sister. "Really? That's a serious accusation. We need to be sure, Ettie. Don't confront her."

"I won't. Why are you always warning me not to confront people."

"I don't know, Ettie, possibly because you always do."

Ettie rolled her eyes. "Just follow my lead."

As they pushed the door open to the small bakery/café, the smell of fresh bread and pastries filled the air, a normally comforting aroma that now seemed tinged with the weight of unanswered questions.

Mrs. Henderson greeted them with her usual warm smile, but it faltered under the sisters' serious expressions. "Ettie, Elsa-May, is there something on your minds?"

Ettie, wasting no time, laid their suspicions before her. "Mrs. Henderson, we know the key was not baked into the bread. It was placed there. Why? Why did you do it."

"Confrontational," Elsa-May whispered to Ettie, trying not to move her lips.

The baker's face paled, her hands clutching the edge of the counter as if for support. After a moment of tense silence, she sighed, a deep, soul-baring sound. "I... I was trying to find the key to his heart."

Ettie stepped forward. "Tell us everything. How did you get the idea to pretend a key was baked into the bread."

"Yes, and what of the poem?" Elsa-May asked.

Mrs. Henderson's eyes filled tears. "I'd known him for years, loved him from afar. He never saw me, not really. Not the way I saw him. He loved his antiques, was always excited about rare finds. I thought... if I could share that with him, show him my interest, maybe he'd see *me*."

Ettie reached out, touching the baker's arm lightly. "But why the deception with the key?"

"I thought it would be a quaint mystery for him to solve, something to make him smile, to make him think of me when he thought of antiques," Mrs.

Henderson explained, wiping her eyes with the back of her hand. "I never imagined it would tie me to his death. After he was found, everything just spiraled out of control, and no one would stop talking about the key and that stupid poem I made up. It was meant to be something just between the two of us to give us something in common."

Elsa-May nodded slowly. "We understand, Mrs. Henderson, but secrets have a way of growing, of getting out of hand."

Mrs. Henderson sighed. "I guess I should tell the detective that the key was all my doing."

"But why was the key stolen?" Ettie asked. "And who did it?"

"I pretended it was stolen. I thought it best. I didn't like the focus on the key and I didn't want the detective to think the key was related to his death."

Elsa-May's mouth turned down at the corners. "Well, I'm afraid it had the opposite effect. Detective Kelly didn't think anything of the key until it was stolen. You'll have to come clean so he can focus on other things now."

"I will do that. Thank you both for being understanding. I feel like a silly old fool. They say there's no fool like an old fool."

Elsa-May reached out and patted her hand. "There's no shame in love. There should be more love in the world."

"Thank you."

When customers came in, Ettie and Elsa-May said their goodbyes and headed out the door, but not before she gave them both a goodie bag of cakes to take home with them.

"Well, Ettie, we're getting closer to the truth. The key had nothing to do with Don's death. Joy might be the killer after all."

Ettie bit her lip. "I'm not sure."

"And, about you saying you are never confrontational…"

"Don't start, Elsa-May. It worked, didn't it?"

Elsa-May nodded. "It did surprisingly.

"Joy might be in jail, but that doesn't mean the case is closed. We need to find the truth and now I can't help thinking about that phone call Don had just before he died."

CHAPTER 32

*T*he late afternoon sun filtered through the curtains as Ettie, Elsa-May, and Ava sat around the old wooden table in the sisters' cozy kitchen, each nursing a cup of tea. The revelation about the key and Mrs. Henderson's unrequited love had added a bittersweet layer of complexity to the case.

"It's a sad thing, love like that," Elsa-May sighed. "To love someone who hardly notices you."

"Yes," Ettie agreed, stirring her tea absentmindedly. "It can lead people to do strange things. But we know now that the key was a gesture of affection, not a clue to her guilt in his death."

"Or anything to do with his death," Elsa-May added.

Ava nodded, then leaned forward, her expression turning serious again. "I'm sorry I haven't been able to help as much as I'd like."

"We know you're busy. It's okay," Ettie said.

"So, what's our next move? We're back to square one with the suspects or do you think Joy is the killer?" Ava asked.

"Tell her, Ettie," Elsa-May urged.

Ava looked over at Ettie. "What is it?"

"There's something that's been bothering me that I haven't told you yet," she began, hesitating as she tried to piece together her thoughts. "When we entered Don's antique store, I noticed the phone was off the hook. It struck me as odd, but everything else overshadowed it at the time."

"Go on," Ava said.

"Yes, and it makes me wonder…" Ettie paused, organizing her thoughts. "Could the killer have been on the phone with him? Maybe it was a diversion—asking him to check something in the backroom where the second person could have been waiting in the backroom with the knife."

Ava's eyes widened as she considered the possibility. "That's a compelling thought. It would mean at least two people were involved. Someone on the phone and another person at the scene. That's a classic distraction technique. One distracts while the other acts."

"We need to find out who called Don at that time. If we could check the phone records…" Elsa-May said.

Ava was already nodding. "Yes, we need to get a hold of the suspects' cell phone records. See who might have called him around the time of his death. It's a long shot, but it's the best lead we have right now."

"Oh, dear," Ettie muttered. "It sounds like another visit to Detective Kelly is needed. I hope he doesn't get upset with me for forgetting about that phone call. He kept asking if there was anything else, even something that we thought was small."

"The downside is the police will have to subpoena the phone records. That typically requires the approval of a judge. That process might not happen overnight," Ava informed them.

"Do you have a better idea, Ava? I know you had friends when you left us and went to college years ago, so any friends working for the phone company?" Elsa-May asked.

"No, but most people use cell phones these days, not the landline phones. All we need is to get their cell phones and have a look at their call logs."

Ettie frowned, staring at Ava. "Whose cell phones?"

"Anyone at all. Anyone you suspect."

"Ah, good idea. But Joy Basket is in jail so we can't get her phone. We can look at Michelle's phone, but her son is overseas somewhere right now. Then there is Zabrik, but it'll be hard to get to his phone."

"That's all very well and good, but how will we get the phones from them? Ava, you'll have to come with us," Elsa-May said.

Ava grimaced. "I'll go along with you, but I won't be touching anyone's phones."

"Good, you can distract them while Ettie does it."

Ettie frowned once again. "Me? Why do I have to do everything? You're better with cell phones, Elsa-May."

"Ah, I suppose that's true, much like I'm better at everything. All right, I'll do it."

CHAPTER 33

Under the guise of a simple social visit, Ettie, Elsa-May, and Ava made their way back to Don's antique store.

As they entered, the bell on the door tinkled, announcing their arrival. Michelle met them with a weary smile—a hint of suspicion perhaps, or merely the weariness of seeing them two days in a row? "Ava, isn't it?" Michelle asked.

"Yes. I'm surprised you remember. It was years ago that I worked here."

Michelle gave a nod, her eyes sweeping over the three of them. "I didn't know you all knew each other."

"We do. We had to bring Ava back here to see all these lovely things we've been telling her about," Elsa-May exclaimed.

Ettie, meanwhile, was less at ease with the deception. She shuffled awkwardly, her gaze darting around as she tried to spot where Michelle might have left her phone.

Ava took charge, steering Michelle toward a grandfather clock. "This piece is just magnificent. Could you tell me something about it?"

Michelle was only too happy to oblige, launching into the detailed history of the clock, her back momentarily turned to the counter where her phone lay.

Seizing the moment, Elsa-May whispered to Ettie, "Now's your chance."

But as Ettie edged toward the counter, her foot caught on the edge of a rug. She stumbled forward, letting out a small yelp as she fell into a conveniently placed pile of folded floor rugs.

"Oh, my!" Elsa-May exclaimed, rushing to her sister's side. "Ettie, are you alright? We must call 911 at once."

Michelle rushed over. "Is she hurt? Do we need to call an ambulance?"

"No, no," Ettie groaned, playing up her distress. "Just a bit of a shock, I think..."

"Here's a phone. I'll just make a quick call," she said, expertly unlocking the phone as Michelle fussed over Ettie.

While pretending to dial, Elsa-May quickly navigated to the call log, her eyes scanning for any calls made around the time of Don's murder. She noted the details with a mental sharpness that came from years of knitting intricate patterns.

Just then, Ettie, deciding her role had reached its limit, miraculously recovered. "Oh, I think I can stand now. No need for that call, Elsa-May. Just helped me realize how much padding I have on me these days."

Elsa-May placed the phone back on the counter. "Too many of Mrs. Henderson's cakes I'd say."

"Are you sure you're alright?" Michelle asked.

"Better than ever." Ettie chirped, dusting herself off.

At that moment, Craig, Michelle's son, entered the shop from the backroom.

The three ladies stood, staring at him.

Michelle turned around to see what they were gawking at. "Oh, Craig, you're here."

Ava stepped forward. "Hi, I'm Ava. We've never met but I worked for your stepfather years ago."

Craig smiled when he saw Ava. "Nice to meet you. Are you into antiques?"

"Absolutely," Ava replied, letting her eyes wander appreciatively over the shelves before returning her gaze to his. "Maybe you could show me some of your favorites? I'd love an expert's insight."

"I'm not an expert, but I've gathered some knowledge over the years." As Craig eagerly began showing her around, pointing out various items, Ava wondered how to get her hands on his phone.

Meanwhile, Ettie and Elsa-May engaged Michelle in conversation to draw her attention away from Ava's activities. Elsa-May suddenly became interested in a dusty old lamp.

Michelle, intrigued by the prospect of a sale, was keen to discuss the lamp's history. As she did, Ettie 'accidentally' spilled her purse, its contents scattering across the floor.

"Oh, my, I'm all thumbs today," Ettie apologized profusely as Michelle bent down to help her gather her things.

Michelle responded with a light chuckle, her initial annoyance fading as she picked up the lamp to say more nice things about it. "This is actually quite a fascinating piece, believe it or not. It's an oil lamp, quite old but well preserved. It dates back to the early 20th century."

Elsa-May, feigning surprise and delight, leaned in closer, her eyes wide with curiosity. "Really? It looks so unique. What's the story behind it? Who owned it and things like that?"

"Well, this lamp was part of a larger estate sale from an old mansion upstate. The family that owned it were quite prominent in their time—industrial magnates. This piece was in their study. Imagine the conversations it has 'heard' over the decades."

Elsa-May nodded enthusiastically, "That's incredible! It's seen a lot of history, then?"

"Absolutely," Michelle continued, warming to the subject. "It's made from brass, and you can still see some engravings. See here?" She pointed to the intricate designs etched around the base. "Most of it is faded, but it would've been beautiful in its day."

Ettie joined the conversation. "It must be worth quite a bit then?"

Michelle smiled, a hint of a salesperson's gleam in her eyes. "To the right collector, definitely. But for me, it's more about the history, the connection to the past."

"You tell the stories so well," Elsa-May complimented, giving Michelle a friendly smile. "It really does add a certain charm to the shop. Do you mind if I buy it? Depending on the price of course."

"Of course you can. This isn't a museum." Michelle showed Elsa-May the price tag.

"I'll take it."

"Excellent. I'll wrap it up for you. If you're ever interested in more pieces like this, let me know. I always come across interesting finds."

"Will do," Elsa-May replied, her mind already spinning with the information they had just surreptitiously confirmed from Michelle's phone. It seemed every piece in the store did indeed have a story, just as the phone had told its own tale.

"Were you involved in the acquiring of these antiques?" Ettie asked Michelle as she wrapped.

"Yes. Every now and again I'd go to estate sales and auctions with Don. When we were talking, which wasn't very often." She tied string around the package and handed it to Elsa-May. "Enjoy your lamp."

"I certainly will and thank you for the wonderful history lesson," Elsa-May said as they headed toward the door with their parcel.

"Anytime, ladies," Michelle called out after them. "Come back anytime you want to hear more stories."

Noticing Ettie and Elsa-May were leaving, Ava said goodbye to Craig, who followed her to the door.

"You know, my father was a Mennonite," Craig told Ava.

Ava turned around to face him. "I heard that. Wasn't he your stepfather, though?"

"Yes, but I still feel he was my father in many ways. I'd love to chat about it over coffee perhaps." He stared at her, smiling.

"I'd love that. I'll put my number in your phone." She held out her hand and he gave her his phone. After quickly typing in a number, Ava quickly accessed his call log, scanning for any calls made around the time of Don's death. Then she handed the phone back to him. "Call me," she said with a smile.

"Guaranteed."

"Come along," Elsa-May looped her arm through Ava's to whisk her away.

"I'll see you soon," Craig yelled out as the three women hurried away.

When they were around the corner of the store, Ava said, "I feel so bad for talking to that man."

"Did you get to see his calls on his phone?" Elsa-May asked.

"I did and he didn't make any calls at that time at all."

Ettie raised her eyebrows. "I saw you giving Craig your number, but you don't have one."

Ava made a face. "I made one up. I just hope that Jeremiah doesn't find out any of this."

"It was all for a good cause. There was no harm in what you did." Ettie looked over at Elsa-May. "What about Michelle's phone?"

Elsa-May quickly glanced over her shoulder to make sure no one was listening. "She made that call. Put it this way, the call was made from her phone. Her phone was used to call the antique store on the day of Don's death right around the time we would've been there. When I was looking at her phone, I looked at the sign on the door and the numbers matched."

Ettie quickly spotted a bus seat and sat down while she absorbed the news and figured out the implications. "So, she, or someone close to her, made the call that distracted Don and possibly sent him to the backroom?"

Elsa-May nodded. "Correct. The backroom where someone was waiting for him."

"What do we do now?" Ava asked.

"Well, we can't tell the detective because then he'll find out we had a look at their phones, and that's probably illegal or something." Elsa-May hung her head. "The things you get me into, Ettie."

Ettie thought for a moment. "We can tell the detective that I just remembered that the receiver, the handle bit, was off the phone when I got there that day."

"Good thinking, Ettie, and we'll let him handle it from there."

Ava agreed. "Yes, and then he might get those phone records and find out for himself. It'll take longer, but I'm guessing Michelle and Craig think they're in the clear. They won't be going anywhere for a while."

$\mathcal{E}$ttie and Elsa-May, with Ava in tow, made their way to the police station. Keeping their newfound knowledge under wraps, they had decided not to reveal that they knew Michelle was the caller on the day of Don's death. They would approach Detective Kelly with another angle—one that wouldn't expose how deeply they had already dug into the case.

Upon arrival, they were shown into Detective Kelly's office, where the familiar clutter of his desk and the faint smell of coffee welcomed them.

Kelly looked up. "Ah good morning. There are three of you today." Kelly pushed aside some of the files on his desk. "Please take a seat."

Ettie took a deep breath, steeling herself for the conversation. "Detective, I remembered something about the day Don was found, something that might help," she began, her voice steady despite the flutter of nerves.

"Oh?" Kelly leaned back.

"Yes, the phone's receiver in Don's shop was off the hook when we arrived. Just before we found him in the backroom," Ettie explained, watching the detective's reaction closely.

Kelly's brow furrowed. "And you think this is significant?"

"I do," Ettie pressed on. "Think about it. The receiver was off the hook, right before we found him. Doesn't that seem like someone was on the phone with him, possibly luring him to the back where..." she trailed off, the implication hanging heavily in the air.

Kelly, however, seemed unconvinced. "It's not uncommon for a phone to be left off the hook, especially in a busy shop. It could have easily been knocked off, or maybe Don was interrupted and didn't place it back properly."

"But what if it wasn't just an oversight?" Ettie persisted, leaning forward. "What if the person on the other end of that call directed him to the backroom for a reason? Maybe the killer used the phone call as a diversion to get him where they wanted."

Kelly paused, considering her words. He tapped his pen against his desk, a sign of his deepening contemplation. "It's a stretch, Mrs. Smith. People use phones in stores all the time. To tie this to the murder without more to go on..."

"But isn't it worth looking into? Maybe the phone records could tell us something more. Who he spoke to could be vital," Ettie said.

Ava spoke for the first time. "Perhaps look into the phone records of your main suspects?"

Kelly sighed, his gaze shifting between the three women. "It makes no sense to me. You're assuming the person who made this mystery call is guilty, but maybe the person who made this call is innocent. I mean, if they were calling him that means they weren't there, right?"

"It's a hunch," Ettie said.

"Alright, I'll admit, it's not much to go on, but I'll do it just to keep you all happy."

"Thank you, Detective," Elsa-May said. "We just want to make sure every possibility is explored."

Kelly nodded. "I'll need some time to get the necessary approvals for accessing those records, but I'll let you know what I find."

As they left the station, the weight of their secret knowledge remained with them, but there was a small triumph in having convinced Kelly to delve deeper into what they believed was not just a trivial detail.

"We did what we could," Ava said quietly as they walked back to her horse and buggy.

"Yes, and now we wait," Ettie replied, her gaze distant. "Let's hope this leads somewhere."

Elsa-May nodded. "It will, Ettie. It has to."

CHAPTER 35

The next morning, Ettie was looking out the window through her binoculars at the birds that had gathered in the front garden.

"I'm glad you've found something to do."

Ettie lowered her binoculars and looked around. "I've been thinking."

"Oh no. What now?"

"So, Ava mentioned that Don had her sign a lot of documents and it made her uneasy, remember?"

"Yes."

"So, when she was no longer there, who would sign all those things for him?"

Ettie shrugged her shoulders and kept knitting. "Perhaps Mrs. Henderson seeing he went there every morning."

"Exactly!" Ettie yelled causing Elsa-May to jump.

"Do you think he got her to sign something to do

with his murder? You're not making sense. Didn't we decide Michelle and her son are the killers?"

"Maybe, but I would like to know what kind of things he got her to sign. What if he was involved in strange financial dealings that implicated Michelle and her son? If we find out, we might be able to provide more proof for Detective Kelly. Coming?" Ettie asked.

Elsa-May looked up. "Where to?"

"I suddenly feel like cake."

Elsa-May rolled her eyes. "What's new? Just let me finish the end of this row."

THE BAKERY WAS FILLED with the familiar comforting aroma of freshly baked goods as Elsa-May and Ettie arrived. They found Mrs. Henderson behind the counter, arranging a display of pastries.

"Morning, Mrs. Henderson," Elsa-May greeted her as they entered.

Mrs. Henderson looked up with a warm smile. "Good morning, dears. What brings you in so early?"

"We were hoping to chat with you," Ettie said, glancing around the bakery. "Seems like a quiet morning."

Mrs. Henderson nodded. "It is now, but I was rushed off my feet a moment ago. Why don't you sit down? I'll bring some cake and coffee."

"Thank you." Elsa-May and Ettie settled at a cozy

corner table, and Mrs. Henderson soon joined them with a tray holding slices of cake and steaming mugs of coffee. She took a seat across from them.

"So, what's on your minds?" Mrs. Henderson asked, taking a sip of her coffee.

Elsa-May leaned forward. "Can I have a bit more milk?"

Mrs. Henderson, sprang to her feet. "Oh yes. I'll get some."

Ettie frowned at Elsa-May. "You're embarrassing. There's already milk in there. I can tell."

"Not enough. See?" Elsa-May offered her cup to show Ettie, but tipped the cup over too far. Coffee went everywhere. "Oh no, Ettie. I'm sorry."

"This is turning into a fiasco. I'll get some napkins." Ettie got up to the counter to find some napkins and didn't see them anywhere. She saw Mrs. Henderson in the backroom talking to someone at the door. Ettie came up alongside her causing Mrs. Henderson to jump.

"I didn't see you there."

"Elsa-May spilled her coffee. Honestly, I can't take her anywhere these days." The delivery man left and Mrs. Henderson closed the door but not before Ettie noticed another door in the lane. "Is that the back door to the antique store?"

"That's right. Don never used it though. He always came through the front. People don't generally come in the back here."

"Oh, I hope I didn't upset you. Ah, here are a couple of napkins." Ettie grabbed a couple of napkins. "So, it's funny that both stores' backrooms are so close, yet they are a long way when you get outside."

"The street curves. That's why." Mrs. Henderson placed her delivery of takeout cups down, grabbed a bottle of milk and headed back to the table.

Elsa-May looked up as they approached. "I'm sorry, but Ettie made a dreadful mess here."

Ettie's mouth fell open. "Me?"

"Yes. If you weren't blabbing on about the milk already being in the tea, I wouldn't have had to show you. If I didn't have to show you, it wouldn't have toppled over."

Ettie sighed as she sat down and proceeded to mop up the spill.

"No matter." Mrs. Henderson chuckled as she slid into her chair while Elsa-May topped off her coffee with more milk. "Now, what do you have to tell me."

"We've been looking into some things about Don. When our friend Ava worked for him years ago, he had her sign some documents when she worked for him. It made us wonder if he ever got you to sign anything," Ettie asked.

Mrs. Henderson's expression shifted, a flicker of unease crossing her face. She set her cup down and sighed. "Yes, he did."

"What kind of documents were they?" Elsa-May asked gently.

"Contracts, delivery receipts, things like that. But there were other documents too. Ones I didn't fully understand. He assured me they were routine, so I trusted him. Why wouldn't I?"

Elsa-May frowned. "So, you never questioned him about them?"

Mrs. Henderson shook her head. "Not really. Don was persuasive, and I was busy with the bakery. I didn't have the time or the energy to delve into the details."

Ettie leaned closer. "Do you still have any of those documents?"

"No. He never left me any copies. He always took them with him. One day…" She took a deep breath. "Recently he had me sign his will."

"That must've been extremely upsetting for you," Elsa-May said.

"It was, he asked me to meet him at his house. I got all dressed up and went to meet him. I thought he was inviting me for supper. When I got there, he produced more paperwork. I found out it was his will. I couldn't believe it."

Ettie frowned at Mrs. Henderson. "It was you?"

She opened her eyes wide. "What was me?"

"You killed him. It all makes sense now. You loved him, but he didn't love you. That made you upset. And when you found out that he was leaving everything to his ex-wife and stepson, that was the last straw. Plus, you saw that he was throwing out all your pastries rather than eating them."

"No, no. You've got it all wrong. I don't know what you're talking about."

"What do you mean, Ettie? She was the keeper of the key. The killer is the person with the key and don't forget the phone call." Elsa-May frowned at Ettie then looked over at Mrs. Henderson. "I'm so sorry. My sister is normally good about these things."

"Let's go now, Elsa-May." Ettie sprang to her feet, but before she got to the door, Mrs. Henderson had locked it and turned over the sign on the door to say 'Closed.' Ettie went to open the door, but it was locked.

"She's got the key," Elsa-May said, noticing Mrs. Henderson slipping the key into her pocket.

Rushing behind the counter, Mrs. Henderson produced a gun. "Now we're going on a little car ride."

"No, we're fine thank you. We were just leaving. Come along, Ettie." Elsa-May stood at the door. "We'll need you to unlock this please."

Mrs. Henderson moved forward and pressed the gun against Elsa-May's head. "I don't think so."

"We'll do what you say," Ettie told her. "Just keep calm. We can talk about this."

"I'm not in the mood for talking." Mrs. Henderson directed them out the backdoor into the lane.

"Are you going to kill us?" Elsa-May asked.

"Only if you don't do exactly what I say. Both of you put out your hands."

They each did as she asked, and from the trunk of her car, Mrs. Henderson took out zip ties. She tied their hands in front of them. Then she opened the back door of her car for them to get in.

"Where are you taking us?" Elsa-May asked.

"I've got something to show you both."

Once in the backseat, Ettie and Elsa-May stared at each other and then Ettie whispered to Elsa-May, "She must've killed him."

"Do you think so?" Ettie whispered back sarcastically.

"Quiet!" Mrs. Henderson said as she started up the motor. They drove in silence for ten minutes and then the car's tires crunched over gravel as it veered onto a lesser-used path, leading to a secluded grassy area surrounded by dense woods.

As the car came to a stop, Mrs. Henderson turned to face them. "You need to understand. I loved him. I just wanted him to notice me." Mrs. Henderson got out and opened one of the back doors. "Out!"

Ettie and Elsa-May complied, stepping out into the chilly air. The ground was damp underfoot, a mist rising slowly around them as the sky got grayer.

CHAPTER 36

"Walk," Mrs. Henderson directed, gesturing with the gun for them to move ahead of her toward a darker patch of the field.

The sisters exchanged a brief, worried glance but did as they were told, each step taking them further from the car and deeper into desolation. They could see now, the outline of a freshly dug pit, its edges rough against the soft earth.

"Is that for us?" Elsa-May's voice was barely a whisper, her fear palpable.

Mrs. Henderson didn't answer, just kept her gun trained on them. "Far enough," she finally said as they neared the hole.

"What is this hole for?" Ettie asked.

"I always like to prepare for any eventuality."

"So, was I right? You saw that he was throwing out your cakes?"

"I couldn't believe it when I saw his small bin in his kitchen cupboard. It was full of things I'd baked with love and given him. He tossed them out as though they were garbage. When he had me sign his will, I saw I was getting nothing. That's what I meant to him —nothing."

Elsa-May, overcome by the surreal horror of the situation, stumbled and fell to her knees. Just as she did so the clouds parted, and the sun shone brightly upon them.

Seizing the moment of distraction, Ettie swiftly turned around, her tied hands clutching her bird watching binoculars. As Mrs. Henderson moved to help Elsa-May, presumably to keep her moving, Ettie angled the binoculars so the sun reflected into Mrs. Henderson's eyes.

Blinded momentarily, Mrs. Henderson cried out and instinctively raised her arm to shield her face. Ettie lunged forward, her heart pounding as she grappled with the older woman for control of the gun. The struggle was brief. Mrs. Henderson was strong, but the surprise and temporary disorientation worked in Ettie's favor.

With a desperate twist, Ettie managed to wrench the gun from Mrs. Henderson's grip and pointed it squarely at her. "Enough," Ettie breathed out, her entire body shaking.

Mrs. Henderson, now the one at gunpoint, stood

frozen, the realization of her loss of control dawning on her hardened features.

"Elsa-May, get up," Ettie called without taking her eyes off Mrs. Henderson. Elsa-May, shaken but unharmed, quickly rose to her feet and moved to her sister's side.

"What now, Mrs. Henderson? Was this the plan all along to kill us?" Ettie's voice was firm, her hold on the gun steady despite the adrenaline coursing through her veins.

Mrs. Henderson's eyes flickered with a mix of anger and despair. "I... I lost everything because of him," she spat bitterly, her posture slumping as the fight went out of her. "We had gotten close at one point. He promised me a partnership, recognition, not just some sideline baker he visited. But in the end, I was nothing more than a signature at the end of his will—a will where I inherited nothing!"

"And you thought murdering him and then us would solve what exactly?" Elsa-May asked.

"I don't know... I didn't think it would go this far," Mrs. Henderson confessed, her voice breaking. "I just wanted him to feel a fraction of the pain I felt."

Ettie, still pointing the gun, nodded slowly, understanding the depths of hurt and betrayal that could drive a person to the edge. "Hurting others wasn't going to heal you, Mrs. Henderson. It just spreads more pain."

A long silence fell over the trio, the only sound the rustle of the leaves and the distant call of a bird. Finally, Ettie told Elsa-May, "Use Mrs. Henderson's phone to call 911."

As Elsa-May walked around trying to get a signal on the phone she found in Mrs. Henderson's car, Mrs. Henderson kicked a fallen branch toward Ettie.

Caught off guard, Ettie instinctively shifted her focus to avoid the branch, and in that split second, Mrs. Henderson lunged forward. The two women grappled fiercely for the gun once more, their struggle chaotic as they stumbled toward the dense edge of the woods nearby.

Amid the scuffle, the gun slipped from Ettie's grasp, landing with a dull thud in the underbrush. Mrs. Henderson, with a burst of adrenaline, shoved Ettie back and made a dive for the gun. She grasped it, her fingers wrapping tightly around the handle, regaining control.

"Back off!" she shouted, her voice ragged with desperation as she pointed the gun at Ettie and Elsa-May.

Elsa-May, her protective instincts kicking in, grabbed Ettie's arm. "Ettie, run!"

They both turned and ran into the undergrowth.

With the gun trained on them, Mrs. Henderson's eyes were wild, her chest heaving. "I can't let you turn me in. You don't understand what it's been like."

"Mrs. Henderson, nobody needs to get hurt," Ettie called out calmly from behind a tree. "We can talk this through. There's still a chance to make things right."

But Mrs. Henderson was beyond reason, her mind clouded by fear and despair. "It's too late for that!" she cried out.

Ettie and Elsa-May turned and ran again, dashing into the thicker undergrowth of the woods. Mrs. Henderson fired a wild shot that echoed sharply through the daylight.

Once they were a safe distance away, hidden by foliage, Ettie pulled out her bird watching binoculars. She scanned the area back toward where they had left Mrs. Henderson, spotting her still figure standing by the clearing. Ettie looked down and saw that Elsa-May still had the phone in her hands.

"Call the police. Tell them exactly where we are and what's happening."

Elsa-May dialed 911, her voice low as she relayed their location and the situation to the dispatcher. "Please hurry, she's armed and dangerous. We're hiding in the woods near the clearing,"

As they waited for the police to arrive, the sisters stayed hidden, watching Mrs. Henderson through the binoculars. The waiting was harrowing, every sound amplified in the daytime stillness, causing them to tense.

When the police finally arrived, Ettie and Elsa-May

felt a wave of relief wash over them. The officers moved quickly, fanning out to surround the area. Detective Kelly, recognizable in his overcoat, led the team.

"Mrs. Henderson! It's Detective Kelly," he called out, his voice authoritative. "Put the gun down and come out with your hands up. There's nowhere to go."

CHAPTER 37

*M*rs. Henderson, still clutching the gun, looked around frantically. Realizing she was surrounded, her shoulders slumped in defeat. She lowered the weapon and dropped it to the ground.

Kelly approached her cautiously, signaling his officers to move in. They swiftly placed her in handcuffs. As they escorted her to a police car, Kelly turned his attention to the woods.

"Ettie, Elsa-May! It's safe to come out now," he called.

The sisters emerged from their hiding place, visibly shaken but unharmed.

Kelly walked over to them. "Are you both alright?"

"We're fine, thanks to you," Ettie replied, her voice trembling slightly.

Elsa-May nodded. "Thank you, Detective Kelly. We didn't know what to do."

Kelly smiled reassuringly. "You never do. That's why you should've listened to me and stayed out of it." Then he looked down at their hands that were still bound. He took out a pocket knife and cut through the ties. "Mrs. Henderson will be taken into custody, and we'll sort everything out. What happened exactly? Tell me from the start."

Ettie recounted the events, from their conversation in the bakery to the struggle in the woods. Kelly listened intently, taking notes.

"You both showed a lot of courage," he said once they finished. "This could have ended much worse."

Ettie and Elsa-May kept rubbing their wrists, glad to be free. "We're just glad it's over," Elsa-May said.

Kelly nodded. "You did well. Go home and get some rest. We'll be in touch if we need anything else. I'll have someone drive you home."

The sisters thanked him again and made their way to a waiting police car. As they were driven home, the adrenaline began to wear off, replaced by exhaustion.

"That was close," Elsa-May murmured.

"Too close," Ettie agreed, looking out the window. "But we made it through."

CHAPTER 38

a couple of days after the harrowing events, the atmosphere in Ettie and Elsa-May's home was considerably lighter. The tension that had gripped them was now replaced by the comforting ritual of preparing for a visit from Detective Kelly.

As they set up the living room, their family cat, Kelly—cheekily named after the detective, despite being a female—wove between their legs, her purring a soft soundtrack to their preparations.

Detective Kelly appeared at their doorway. "Anyone home?"

Recognizing the voice, Elsa-May called out, "We've been expecting you. Come in."

"I can't thank you two enough for your help," he said, settling into an armchair with the steaming cup of coffee Elsa-May had just handed him, while Ettie offered cream and sugar. "Mrs. Henderson eventually made a full confession, and we were able to release Joy Basket."

"I'm so pleased everything is resolved," Ettie said.

The cat, perhaps sensing the importance of the visitor, jumped onto the detective's lap, curling up contentedly. Detective Kelly chuckled, held his coffee in one hand and stroked the cat with the other. "I must say, it's quite an honor to have such a charming namesake. Although I don't like pets, this one is okay."

Their laughter was interrupted by Snowy, who bounded into the room, his tail wagging furiously. Ettie led him to a bedroom where he could settle down without causing further chaos.

Once Snowy was content with a chew toy and safely out of the way, Ettie returned to the living room.

Detective Kelly sipped his coffee thoughtfully. "It's fascinating, isn't it? How appearances can be so deceptive. Mrs. Henderson seemed so innocent."

"I've never been so scared in my life as I was in that field. I thought our lives were over." Elsa-May's bottom lip quivered.

Ettie nodded, glancing over at the bird watching binoculars resting on a nearby shelf. "Indeed. Who would have thought that something from Don's antique store would end up saving our lives?"

"It's true," Elsa-May agreed.

"And to think," Ettie added, with a mischievous

glance at her sister, "someone once told me to stop wearing those binoculars all the time."

Elsa-May nodded. "I wonder who that could've been."

Ettie laughed. "Well, I'm certainly glad I didn't listen."

Detective Kelly smiled, placing his coffee cup on the table. "It's a good reminder that we often overlook the ordinary tools at our disposal, thinking they're just that —ordinary. Yet, in the right hands, at the right moment, they're anything but. It was a stroke of inspiration to dazzle Mrs. Henderson with the reflection of the lenses of your binoculars, Mrs. Smith."

Ettie gave a nod. "Well, I had a lot of motivation to get away from her. We've got a lot more living to do, haven't we, Elsa-May?"

"Correct. Now, something is puzzling me. Tell me, Detective Kelly, how did Mrs. Henderson find the time to kill him? We were at her bakery and when we left there, we went straight to see him."

"Well, after you walked out, she slipped out of her door and into his. And you having just seen her gave her an alibi. She was a fast thinker. She even had bought a dagger from Don's store just days before his death. She told us she bought it to kill him."

"We never suspected her, not for one minute," Elsa-May said.

"Not until the end when we were talking to her

about signing things. And, I saw how close the back door of the bakery and the back door of the antique store were."

Kelly nodded. "Correct, and the man had some dubious dealings and was always looking for people to sign documents. Nothing too serious. Anyway, Joy Basket was delighted when we let her go. She was shocked about Mrs. Henderson as well. She thought it might have been the stepson."

"It must be a relief for Joy," Ettie said.

"It was, and another thing I must tell you." Kelly grinned as though he was pleased with himself.

Ettie leaned forward. "What's that?"

"I finally got those phone records we talked about. Michelle, the victim's ex-wife had been on the phone to him around the time of his death. So, when you picked up that receiver, Mrs. Smith, Michelle was on the other end of the line."

Ettie nodded, keeping to herself that they already knew the call had come from Michelle's phone. "Interesting."

Kelly frowned at her. "You don't seem surprised."

"Nothing surprises me anymore. I wonder why she hung up on me though. That wasn't very nice."

"She said she heard someone say hello and then she hung up, not knowing what was going on. This is how it all played out," Kelly explained. "When you left the bakery, Mrs. Henderson hurried out her back door and slipped into the antique store. I'm guessing you ambled along taking your time?"

Ettie shrugged. "We went at our usual pace."

"Exactly. So, she entered the back room of the antique store, found him there. According to Michelle, she had asked him to look up where he had got a particular item so we know he was in the backroom. Of course, Mrs. Henderson wouldn't have known he was going to be there, conveniently in the back room, but she would've had enough time to lure him there if the need had arisen."

Ettie tried to wrap her mind around it. "Well, why didn't Michelle tell you about that phone call way back at the beginning? For all she knew, she might've been talking with her husband's killer."

Kelly nodded. "I pointed that out to her. She told me she must've been in so much shock over his death, that it left her mind completely. I do believe her. I could see the memory coming back when I confronted her with the phone records."

"I was right, Ettie. I said he was in the backroom getting information for the person on the phone."

"No. You said he was doing something with a layaway. There was no layaway."

"I was close."

Kelly raised his eyebrows and looked between the two of them. "Can I continue?"

"Oh, I thought you'd finished. Go ahead." Elsa-May gave him a nod.

"Seeing he was stabbed in the back, he might not have heard her approach. So she stabbed him and fled the scene. She changed out of her soiled apron into a fresh one and carried on as though nothing had happened."

Elsa-May sighed. "I can't believe that we were so close. We might've even been inside his store while it was happening in the backroom."

"It's a possibility," Kelly said.

"That explains a lot, but did you ever find out what Ettie saw Joy handing Zabrik that day?" Elsa-May asked.

"Yes. It was a locket that she bought in a mixed lot at an auction. Zabrik's photo was in it. She thought it might be sentimental to him, and it was. Turns out it was his dear departed mother's locket," Kelly said.

Elsa-May's eyes widened. "So, it was a locket that had sentimental value and not a key?"

"Exactly," Kelly replied.

Ettie grinned. "I was right about it being small and shiny."

"Another interesting thing is that we learned from the victim's medical records he was in the early stages of dementia."

"Ettie, that would explain why he didn't remember Ava used to work for him. I think I suggested that."

"I don't recall you saying that. I would've remembered."

Detective Kelly leaned back, a thoughtful look on

his face. "You know, I was suspicious of Mrs. Henderson from the start."

The sisters both looked at him, surprised. "Really? What made you suspect her?" Elsa-May asked.

"It was a small detail, but it stood out to me. When we first spoke with her, she mentioned the exact time Don had come in that morning when she told him about the key. Then she told me the exact time he came back with the both of you the next day. Now, why would she feel the need to tell me that? It was almost like she was establishing a timeline. She was too precise, almost rehearsed. Most people in a state of shock wouldn't remember such exact details without hesitating."

"That was clever of you," Elsa-May said. "Ettie noticed that Don had a trashcan full of pastries and cakes. She kept that in the back of her mind because it was so unusual to waste good food. Then when we were talking to Mrs. Henderson about her signing papers, she mentioned she was in his apartment."

"And she saw the cakes in the trash?" Kelly asked.

"Exactly," Ettie replied. "As well as that, she was signing the will and realized she was getting nothing. He didn't love her, her cakes, or her pastries."

Kelly nodded. "You're correct. She confessed as soon as she read the will, she knew she had to kill him."

Elsa-May thought about that for a moment. "That's unusual for someone to kill someone when they *aren't* in a will. Don't most people kill when they *are* named in a will and they want to hurry things along?"

"Emotions run deep. You'd be surprised what people are capable of when the right chord is struck. A crime of passion," Kelly stated. "Love can quickly turn to hate."

"Did you see my lovely lamp I got from Don's store, Detective?" Elsa-May gestured toward the lamp.

He looked over at the side table near the door. "It looks pretty old."

"I just haven't had time to clean it yet," Elsa-May said. "It'll come up as good as new."

"Don't listen to her," Ettie said. "The lamp is older than she is and that—"

"I wouldn't say anything else if I were you, Ettie. You're not that far behind me in age."

Detective Kelly grinned. "I should go. Nice, lamp, Mrs. Lutz, and keep those binoculars close, Mrs. Smith," Kelly said with a grin. "And not just for bird watching."

As he stood up and prepared to leave, the sisters followed him to the door. Then they stood at their doorway and watched Detective Kelly get into his car.

Ettie looked down at the binoculars and placed them around her neck. "What do you think about my binoculars now that they saved our lives?"

"I have no words." Elsa-May simply shook her head, walked back into the house, sat down, and resumed her knitting.

Unfazed, Ettie picked up her bird-watching binoculars and watched the detective's car until it disappeared into the distance.

Thank you for reading Dial M for Mennonite.

For a downloadable series reading order of all Samantha Price's books, scan below or head to: SamanthaPriceAuthor.com

ALL SAMANTHA PRICE'S SERIES

Amish Maids Trilogy

Amish Love Blooms

Amish Misfits

The Amish Bonnet Sisters

Amish Women of Pleasant Valley

Ettie Smith Amish Mysteries

Amish Secret Widows' Society

Expectant Amish Widows

Seven Amish Bachelors

Amish Foster Girls

Amish Brides

Amish Romance Secrets

Amish Christmas Books

Amish Wedding Season

Shunned by the Amish

Amish Recipe Books (Non-fiction)
Spiral Bound Amish Recipe Books

Stand alones:
The Unwanted Amish Twin

Amish Herbal and Natural Remedies (Non-fiction, Hardcover only)

ABOUT SAMANTHA PRICE

Samantha Price is a USA Today bestselling and Kindle All Stars author of Amish romance books and cozy mysteries. She was raised Brethren and has a deep affinity for the Amish way of life, which she has explored extensively with over a decade of research.

She is mother to two pampered rescue cats, and a very spoiled staffy with separation issues.

www.SamanthaPriceAuthor.com

Made in the USA
Coppell, TX
04 October 2024

38158544R10146